PHANTOM OF BURLAP HALL

Virginia Ironside really enjoys writing about Burlap Hall, finding it a complete and welcome release from her job as an agony aunt for the *Sunday Mirror*. "You can write things in books that you wouldn't ever condone on the problem page," she says. "With fantasy you can be as naughty as you like. You can have villains and horrible things happening, and if it all adds to the plot, that's great." Her intention is simply to write a "good read".

Phantom of Burlap Hall is the third title featuring the staff and pupils of a fusty old boarding school, following *Vampire Master* and *Spaceboy at Burlap Hall*. The author is currently working on a fourth about a poltergeist. Virginia Ironside has also written three novels for adults and two popular stories for younger readers, *Roseanne and the Magic Mirror* and *The Human Zoo*, both published by Walker Books.

Virginia Ironside lives in west London with her teenage son.

PHANTOM OF BURLAP HALL

VIRGINIA IRONSIDE

WALKER BOOKS
LONDON

First published 1991 by Walker Books Ltd
87 Vauxhall Walk, London SE11 5HJ

© 1991 Virginia Ironside
Cover illustration © 1991 Mick Brownfield

This edition published 1992

Printed and bound in Great Britain by
Cox and Wyman Ltd, Reading, Berkshire

British Library Cataloguing Publication Data
A catalogue record for this book
is available from the British Library.

ISBN 0-7445-2319-2

For Gemma Woodward

CHAPTER ONE

As Mr Fox, the headmaster of Burlap Hall, gloomily shuffled bits of paper around his desk, he wondered what complete prat had ever decided to call the first term of the year the "spring" term. The term that began in January actually *ended* at the beginning of the spring. You'd be lucky to see so much as a snowdrop before the first week of the holidays. It should be called the "winter" term, he decided. And in fact this year it should have been called the "incredibly-freezing-cold-icy-covered-with-snow" term.

Certainly, by the day term began, the cold had already wreaked enough damage on the school building. Snow had nestled cunningly in the old gutters, causing leaks all over the top floor. Mr Fox had actually been reduced to hopping up on the roof in his dressing gown with a broom to sweep off the stuff – feeling a complete wally, especially when the postman had waved up at him and yelled, "Bit late this year, eh, Santa?" His toes still hadn't recovered from the experience.

The new science block, his pride and joy – well, the new science block could barely be seen for snow. Only small sections of the windows peeped out from under a veil of ice; the satellite dish on the top was bent with the weight of snow, tipped lopsidedly like a spilled bowl of ice-cream.

As for the sports centre, frost had ruined the electrics of the brand new heated swimming pool and the whole thing had frozen, trapping a stray rubber bathing hat in the middle like a fly in amber. The nets on the tennis courts were laden with snow, and icicles dripped from the cracked guttering round the roofs. The damage caused had been extensive and as a result, facing the headmaster on his desk, was a great pile of bills for repairs.

"Pessimissimus," he muttered to himself. When those mysterious spaceboys had come last year and their parents had refurbished the entire school in one day, he'd thought his troubles were over. But after this winter, things at Burlap Hall were pretty much the same as they always had been. Disastrous.

A knock on the door announced Mr Fritz, the science master. In his hairy suit and his dilapidated spectacles, he looked every bit the mad professor.

"Cup of tea, Headmaster?" he enquired. "I'm just making one for the drains men. They've fixed the blockage, by the way."

"What blockage?" asked Mr Fox irritably. "There never used to be one."

The men from Drain-O-Cure ("All drain problems solved – we remove all blockages from your waste pipes.") had been in all morning "rodding" the drains (whatever that meant) and asking for cups of tea.

"Probably something in the side of the drain dislodged by the sudden rush of water when the pipes unfroze during the brief thaw," said Mr Fritz. "You see," he added, putting his fingertips together and closing his eyes in a way that filled Mr Fox with a sense of impending doom, "when you weigh the volume of water and multiply it by the speed of its passage, taking into account the diameter of the drain, you have to divide this by the difference between the temperature of the water and that of the drain surface. Thus the speed is increased to a level which defies the volume capacity and may combine to dislodge any loose matter – and it doesn't take a genius to realize that this invariably results in a blockage."

Mr Fox stared at him with bulging eyes. Why did people always start these kinds of explanations with the words, "You see..."? He didn't see at all. But he said, in a voice full of weary confidence, "You don't have to explain that to *me*."

Mr Fritz handed Mr Fox the bill. "Afraid they seem to have the same skills for removing money from your bank account as they do for removing blockages from the drains," he said as he saw Mr Fox's face fall.

Mr Fox put his head in his hands. "Don't give them tea," he complained bitterly. "At these rates they can afford to buy their own."

Before he left, Mr Fritz's eye was caught by an outstanding bill in Mr Fox's "pending" tray. It was from Trustus Insurance, typed in red; the insurance policy for the science block was overdue. He coughed discreetly, pointing questioningly at the document.

"They can wait for their money," said Mr Fox angrily. "I just haven't got it. Nothing's going to happen to it. It's hardly likely to be struck by lightning in this weather. Or be set on fire, come to that."

Mr Fritz hesitated. "But we've had so many more applications for pupils to the school as a result of it. Surely it's worth protecting? I mean – you never know. Anything could happen."

As the science teacher, Mr Fritz dearly loved the new science block and had cut his holidays short so that he could spend a few days pottering around in it on his own.

Mr Fox sighed and spread out his hands. "I've got enough bills!" he said. "And I've just paid for this wretched Paris trip for the fourth form. If you want, you pay for it."

"All right," said Mr Fritz eagerly. He took the bill, pulled out his cheque book, wrote a cheque and stuffed everything into an envelope. "I'll post it now," he said. "Just to be on the safe side."

"Excellent," said Mr Fox irritably. "Now if

you'll excuse me, I've got a lot to get on with."

And as Mr Fritz shut the door, Mr Fox took a copy of *The Sun* from his bottom drawer, removed a bottle of whisky from behind a bookshelf, poured a large tot into his inkwell and settled down to a good old read until teatime.

While Mr Fox was "getting on with things", his pupils were making their way from all over the country to gather at Burlap Hall for the beginning of term.

"Well, at least it's a short term," said Tom, counting the weeks in the new diary he'd been given for Christmas. He was sitting in a steamy train compartment at a tea-stained table with his two friends, Miles and Susan. There was nothing in the diary yet except his parents' birthdays, his hamster's birthday (well, near enough), his own birthday (in red) and nine dates which read, variously, "Term starts", "Term ends" and "Half-term". The diary people had already written in "Christmas Day" which was a bit of a disappointment.

Miles rubbed a patch of the window with the sleeve of his school blazer. "Look at that!" he said, pointing to the snow-covered fields that fled by outside. "At least we can go sledging."

"If they let us," said Susan, looking up from a copy of a book called *Rights for Kids!* that her brother had given her for Christmas. "Did you know that at five years old you're allowed to drink alcohol at home?"

"So presumably you could be an alcoholic at six," said Miles. "Great."

"But isn't that just the law in the States?" asked Tom, knowing Susan was American.

"No, it's an English book," said Susan, looking at the spine.

"When are you allowed to leave school, more importantly?" asked Miles.

Susan looked in the index. "Oh, here ... not until sixteen, I'm afraid," she said. "Hey, then you can also hold a licence to drive an invalid carriage or a mowing machine! *And* you can buy liqueur chocolates ... and you can sell scrap metal!"

"Let's look at that," said Miles, taking it. "Oh, look, the last entry – at twenty-one you can apply for a licence to sell alcohol!"

"To five year olds probably," said Tom.

"No," said Susan, taking the book back and looking through it, "because you're not allowed to buy alcohol until you're eighteen."

Miles grabbed it back. The usual bickering between Miles and Susan had already begun. Tom swung his feet as the train chuntered on.

On the other side of the carriage Asquith Minor was showing off an electronic game he'd got for Christmas, while Sheila, next to him, was embroidering a tapestry in big fat pink wool.

"You going on the Paris trip?" Tom asked Susan.

"No, because I've just come from there. My parents have been posted from the States to the American Embassy there," said Susan. "I wish I were going back, though."

"I'm going," said Miles. "It'll be good fun. It's this week, isn't it? Seems hardly worth unpacking at school when we get there."

"It's some off-season deal that Mr Fox fixed up," said Tom gloomily. "Specially cheap because no one else in their right minds wants to go at this time of year. It'll be so cold in Paris we'll freeze, the Eiffel Tower will be closed and Notre Dame will be covered in snow."

"Still, it'll be good fun," said Miles.

"Which is one thing we won't be having this term," said Susan.

"Let's hope this term is a normal, peaceful one, for once," said Tom, thinking back on their previous adventures at Burlap Hall.

"I couldn't take any *more* strange happenings," said Miles. "I think I'd almost rather take exams."

"We've had more than our fair share of drama already," said Susan. "And statistics show..."

"Stuff statistics," said Tom cautiously. "We shouldn't be talking like this. We're tempting fate."

"Boys!" said Susan, tossing her frizzy red

hair contemptuously. "You think that girls are so superstitious, but in fact it's always the guys who are the ones who touch wood and won't walk under ladders. I'm telling you. There's nothing to worry about. This term is going to be the most boring term in history."

"Don't you mean herstory?" asked Miles, cheekily, knowing how seriously Susan took women's rights.

Susan pouted, refusing to be drawn.

"You're mental," she said, going back to her book. Tom thought of saying "womental" but decided against it.

Having paid some of the bills (and put the rest into his "pending" tray), Mr Fox greeted the other teachers who had gathered at the school throughout the morning. Before the first pupils arrived for tea, he took his gown from the cupboard and shook it out. He always wore it on the first day, to impress the parents. He was about to leave his study to go downstairs when there was a tap at his door.

"Come in," he said.

But the door remained shut.

"Signor Ruzzi?" he asked. Signor Ruzzi, the fiery music teacher, was the only teacher who hadn't yet got to the school. Mr Fox dreaded his arrival, as he always had a complaint about the state of the piano. It had got hot and dried out, or it had got damp and warped or mice had gnawed at the strings. Last term he'd complained that middle C was too flat, but Mr Fox thought that was going too far. Whoever wanted bumpy notes? They'd be so difficult to play.

But there was no sign of Signor Ruzzi and at the next knock Mr Fox jumped up angrily and opened it. And as he did so, he was struck by a horrible sensation. There was nothing but a gust of cold, dank air outside, as if someone from a recently-opened grave had stood there just a minute before. Mixed with this dank smell was the faint whiff of – of all things – drains.

Mr Fox peered out into the corridor which, for early afternoon, seemed surprisingly dark. Then suddenly, from out of nowhere, a sheet of paper was thrust into his hand.

He returned to his office and stared at the piece of paper. Or was it paper? It seemed more like parchment. On it, in crabbed black handwriting, was written this sinister note:

IMPOSTER! it started. *You know nothing of schooling or of teaching boys and girls! I have been waiting for over a century to claim my rightful place! Now, the spell has been broken! Meet me outside the school doors at midnight! If you fail to make the appointment, great disaster will befall the school. Till midnight!*

Yours,

The Phantom

Well! thought Mr Fox. If this was meant to be a joke he'd like to tell the prankster what he thought of him. If it wasn't one thing it, was another. In the holidays it was repairs and bills and in the term-time it was boys and girls, and their dreadful behaviour.

From his window he noticed the first bus-load of pupils crunching into the drive. Mr Fox tore the note into tiny shreds and threw it away. True, he hadn't been aware of there being any pupils around until this first coachload, but one of them must have been dropped off earlier to have performed this ridiculous caper. The term had well and truly started. Sighing, Mr Fox made his way to the assembly hall.

For the children, the first day of term progressed like the first day of every other term. The usual disgusting tea, the usual mooching about on the first evening because there was no homework to do, the usual unpacking and organizing of rooms, the usual air of excitement in catching up with everyone's news, all mingled with the slight gloom of knowing that they were going to be stuck together day and night for the next couple of months.

The only difference on that particular day was a meeting held for the pupils going on the Paris trip. Mr Carstairs (English and games) and Miss Shepherd (cookery and crafts) were the teachers accompanying the group and they insisted that the twelve who were going all meet in the common room at seven o'clock.

"Now, since we're leaving the day after tomorrow, I hope you have your passports!" fluted Miss Shepherd, who launched the meeting. This was clearly her idea of a joke as she paused expectantly for laughter which never came. Finally Asquith Minor and Rosemary obliged with polite giggles. Mr Carstairs continued.

"We're going to Paris for three reasons," he said. "One, because it's just bursting with culture and has some absolutely, er, brill pictures there, like the *Mona Lisa*, with her famous smile, not to mention Notre Dame of Hunchback fame and the Pompidou Centre and Montmartre..."

"Way-hey!" whispered Miles to Tom, leering. "The red-light district!"

"What's a red-light district?" asked Tom.

"It's the naughty place – strip clubs, girls..." Miles rolled his eyes. "Zizi, Fifi, *Folies Bergère*, can-can dancers..." He made sexy curving signs in the air.

Tom felt a bit nervous. Much as he wanted to look around he hoped Miles wouldn't try to drag him off anywhere funny.

"Secondly," continued Mr Carstairs, "because it will improve your French no end. And as we'll be travelling around all over the

17

place, I want you all to be particularly well-behaved..."

"And polite to the Frogs," added Miles, grinning.

"Except," said Mr Carstairs, "I don't think you should call them Frogs."

"Frogs," piped up Miss Shepherd, her red nose pinkening in her pale fragile face, "are sweet things which live in ponds."

("Slimy, like French people," muttered Miles darkly to Tom. Tom started to dread the trip. He was sure Miles would get them into trouble by awful kind of racist talk.)

"Remember," added Miss Shepherd, "you are all ambassadors for England. Your good behaviour should be in complete contrast to the ... er..."

"Yobs," helped Mr Carstairs kindly. "And lager-louts."

"Yobs," enunciated Miss Shepherd carefully, as if just mentioning the word were like drinking poison. "Any questions?"

"*Non!*" shouted Miles. "*Allons-y!*"

"I wish I were going with you," said Susan later when she popped into their bedroom for a quick gossip after supper. "You'll love it."

"*I* wish you were coming, too," said Miles mournfully.

"You haven't seen my book, by the way?" she asked, looking round the room.

18

"No – you mean *Rights for Kids!* Why should we want that?"

"I had it on the bus but I haven't seen it since I unpacked."

"Are you still sharing with Rosemary?" asked Tom, as he finished his unpacking.

"Yes, worst luck," said Susan. "She's still into ballet. Last term she kept doing arabesques before we went to sleep and knocking all my stuff off the mantelpiece. Or she'd twirl about pretending to be a dying swan. It's so embarrassing."

"Maybe she's got your *Rights for Kids!* book, eh?" said Tom.

"Rosemary," declared Susan, "wouldn't know a right for a kid if it were presented to her on a plate roasted with chips and peas."

The first day back always left everyone, including the teachers, exhausted, so by ten o'clock most of the school had bedded down and was preparing for sleep – including Mr Fox.

He had thought no more about the sinister letter he'd received earlier in the day and at five to twelve was snoring loudly in his bed, unaware that it might have been wiser had he responded a little more positively to his mysterious correspondent.

Midnight came. Midnight went. Then, at five past midnight, the still, cold night was broken by a rumbling sound like a crack of thunder which shook the night air. The huge silhouette of the brand new science block, the pride and joy of Burlap Hall, shook slightly and shivered as if it were cold. Then, with a dreadful shudder and a great cloud of smoke and dust, the whole building collapsed with a mighty crash into its snowy foundations. Gone were the gleaming windows and the satellite dish that glittered on top; gone were the wide and airy laboratories, the science stores, the classrooms.

Nothing was left of the science block but an enormous, smoking pile of bricks and broken glass. And through the smoke drifted a smell. A pervading smell of old graves. And drains.

CHAPTER TWO

Tom never slept well on the first night of term and tonight was no exception. He woke at six o'clock feeling homesick and wondering if his mum had remembered to feed his hamster. Miles was still asleep in the other bed in their room, so he couldn't have a chat but if he lay in bed any longer he knew he'd start feeling really gloomy. So he got up and pottered round the room, looking for an Asterix to take his mind off things. Passing the window, he pressed his nose against the pane and looked out.

My goodness, how cold it was! His nose felt frozen just from touching the glass. As his breath iced up on the window, he rubbed at the white frost and stared out. In the January dawn he could barely make out the trees, the lawn, the tennis courts – but then he looked again.

Where was the science block?

Lifting the window as quietly as he could, and shivering as the bitter air cut into the room, Tom leaned out of the window.

But there was no sign of the building.

He blinked several times. Then he spotted the vast pile of rubble where the science block had once been, still smoking with the dust from the crash.

Gingerly easing the window down so as not

to make a sound, Tom frowned. He must tell *someone*. He pulled on his dressing gown, tugged on his baggy Swedish slippersox (a present from his auntie at Christmas) and tiptoed from the room.

"Sir? Sir?" Tom knocked on Mr Fritz's door.

"Come in! Come in!" Mr Fritz was already awake and sitting on his bed, which was piled high with weird bits of laboratory equipment, half-unpacked suitcases, clothes and calculation tables. He was packing the bowl of his first pipe of the day and, dressed in his hairy dressing gown, which looked as if it had been made from the same material as his only suit, he looked more like a crazy old hedgehog than ever.

"Popped in for a morning cuppa?" he asked cheerfully, gesturing to the kettle gurgling on top of a precarious pile of old science books on his desk. "Feeling a bit 'first-day-of-termish'? Can't say I blame you. Feel a bit like that myself, even though I am four times your age."

"Thanks a lot – but no," said Tom. "It's the science block. Have you seen it?"

"Science block, science block?" Mr Fritz laughed. "Tall building, best in the country, most up-to-date laboratory in the whole of England, pride and joy of Burlap Hall? Yes, I think I can say I've seen the science block!"

"When did you last see it?" insisted Tom.

"Oh dear, so it's a hanging matter, eh?" asked Mr Fritz jokingly, getting up to switch off the kettle.

"No, what I mean is, have you seen it *today*?" asked Tom.

Mr Fritz looked puzzled. "Why? Has it grown? What's happened?"

Tom cleared his throat. "It seems to have collapsed, sir," he said.

Mr Fritz's expression changed at once. He tugged at his dressing-gown cord and pulled a tighter knot.

"It can't have collapsed," he said frowning. "It was fine yesterday."

"Yes, it was fine yesterday."

"But today?" Mr Fritz looked at Tom questioningly. Tom shook his head. "Well, let's go and have a look."

Together they hurried down the corridors to the main hall and Mr Fritz unlocked the huge oak doors of the school. Stepping outside into the crisp darkness, his slippered feet crunched in the snow; then, blinking to adjust his eyes, he stared at where the science block used to be. His eyes travelled down the empty black sky to the huge pile of bricks and rubble – all that was left of the pride and joy of Burlap Hall.

Then suddenly, in the middle of the snow, the science teacher burst into tears.

"Oh, sir, oh, sir!" said Tom, full of

23

consternation and embarrassment. He didn't know what to do, but he put an arm round Mr Fritz's prickly dressing gown. "Don't worry. I'm sure it can be mended. It could be rebuilt, surely, I mean – oh dear, please don't be so upset. I wish I could do something. I didn't mean to upset you... Shall I get Mr Fox?"

Mr Fritz stumbled backwards into the hall, sat on a bench and tried to recover. He gave an enormous sniff and shook his head like a dog.

"I'm so sorry," he said. "Shock. The cerebral cortex reacts on the hypothalamus which in turn causes a nervous reaction in the tearducts. Nothing more to it than that." He rubbed his eyes with a hairy sleeve.

"Ridiculous behaviour," he said to himself. "After all, it's only a science block." Then he burst into tears again.

Tom felt so worried that he could have cried himself. But Mr Fritz recovered more quickly this time.

"I'll find Mr Fox," he said, in a rather croaky voice, getting up. "Don't worry. No doubt the insurance ... oh dear, oh dear. The structural foundations ... the bills ... what a terrible, *terrible* tragedy."

The whole school was stunned by the disaster. Not a single person had heard it happen – and yet everyone felt threatened by the smouldering heap of stones and glass that lay like some gigantic tombstone in the school grounds.

After breakfast, mounds of toast and trays of cereal and yoghurt sat untouched, since so few people felt like having more than a bite.

In his geography lesson, Mr Roy started explaining about earthquakes and how they were made and then paused, chalk in hand. "Or perhaps you'd like to tackle another subject today," he said. "I don't want to worry you."

"It couldn't have been an earthquake, could it, sir?" asked Asquith Minor.

"No," said Mr Roy. "We don't have earthquakes here."

But everyone noticed that Mr Roy, a vegetarian who lived mainly on a diet of sunflower seeds that he picked at during lessons, left his usual pot of them untouched that day.

Mr Fritz had to cancel his science lessons because he felt so shocked by the catastrophe. Miss Shepherd insisted on bringing a chair to the cookery lessons, which she moved from stove to stove in the kitchens as she supervised everyone's culinary efforts, because she "felt so wobbly".

Before starting a history lesson on the fall of Rome, Mrs Grain gulped a bit and said, "Oh dear. Not the best topic to tackle today, is it? Let's look at Renaissance man instead."

And during the music lesson Signor Ruzzi suddenly said, "Thanka goodness my new piano eet ees not in the science block!"

"New piano?" asked Sheila, who was sitting in front.

"No, eez vairy vairy old. But fed up I am with the olda piano here. Too sharp. Too flat. Not enough – mmm!" He gestured in the air. "I my special home piano have transported here for thees term, my piano on which my father taught me to playa and on which my father's father taught heem to playa, and on which my father's father's father taught heem to playa, on which my..."

Luckily Simon burst out laughing which stopped the flow.

"So where is it?" asked Miles.

"My piano eet ees parked in the barn until tomorrow when we swap it with the school one."

"Parked?" said Miles. "You mean you *drove* it here?"

The idea of Signor Ruzzi astride his piano racing along the M1 ("With his feet on the pedals, one the accelerator, one the brake!" chuckled Tom.) made everyone laugh, even Signor Ruzzi, and briefly the tension was broken. But even so, there was a nervousness that pervaded the whole school. And certainly no one particularly wanted to look out of the windows, and if they went outside they tried to take a detour. The sight of the heap of rubble was too depressing. And really rather frightening. Because what would have happened, everyone was thinking, if *someone had actually been inside the building at the time*? It was too horrible to think about.

"I'm so glad we're going to Paris tomorrow, aren't you?" said Tom to Miles.

Mr Fox was the most affected of all. What he just couldn't understand was how it had happened. When it had been constructed he'd seen the building go up with his own eyes, witnessed the iron girders being rammed into the ground, seen the very foundations being laid. If just the top had fallen off he could have understood it. But everything – ! There was not one stone left standing.

The only consolation was that he'd had the foresight to renew the insurance. It was jolly lucky, he said to himself, that he was such an efficient and sensible chap and had insisted only yesterday that Mr Fritz post off the policy. But even so, it would be at least a term before the block could be rebuilt.

"Oh, pessimissimus!" he moaned over a steaming cup of coffee in his study. "What a life!"

A knock on the door announced Mr Fritz with the post. Mr Fox looked up at him dolefully. "What a way to start the term," he sighed, shuffling through the brown envelopes and bills. "Hey – hang on! What's this?" Mr Fox held out a piece of paper that seemed to have slipped in among the envelopes. "How did this get here? There's no envelope and no stamp."

Mr Fritz took it and unfolded it.

THE FIRST DISASTER HAS STRUCK! he read. *See what happens when you don't keep your appointments? Tonight. Midnight. Or else.*

Yours,

The Phantom

The science teacher didn't notice the colour drain from Mr Fox's face. "What on *earth*...? Hmm. Parchment," he added, looking closely at the paper. "Curious. What was this appointment?"

With a trembling hand Mr Fox pulled his wastepaper basket towards him and retrieved the torn fragments of yesterday's letter. He showed it to Mr Fritz.

The science teacher sat down. "This must be some kind of a joke," he said eventually, after reading both letters. He turned the pieces of paper over in his hand. "It's not difficult to fake these kinds of things, you know. You just soak an ordinary piece of paper in water in which you have dissolved a few grains of instant coffee, leave it in a warm place, and then the air activates the dye, lightening it as it dries, giving the impression of old parchment.

28

Easily explained. Some joker wrote the first one – and when the science block fell down he wrote the second. Just a coincidence. But who is the culprit?"

"I'd give anything to get my hands on him. Or her," said Mr Fox, furiously.

Physical education was not Tom's idea of fun. Swimming in the new pool was OK, but exercises and press-ups were another matter. It was all very well for Mr Carstairs; he went jogging every day and was so fit his muscles bubbled all over his body. But Tom always felt like a worn-out sock when it came to leaping over a vaulting horse or wading into a pool. Rosemary, being a ballet dancer, could do every single exercise, and even a pirouette in mid-air as she leapt up and down on the trampoline. Miles managed to struggle through his gymnastics without attracting attention, and Asquith Minor always seemed to have a very good excuse not to take part – he'd got a cold or he'd twisted his ankle. But Tom, as Mr Carstairs constantly told him, was not a co-ordinated boy.

"Co-what?" asked Tom, breathlessly, trying in vain to keep upright as he bounced on the trampoline.

"Co-ordinated," said Mr Carstairs, "means all your limbs working in harmony with one another." The sports teacher sprang on to the floor and started doing press-ups, his green track-suit wobbling as he lifted himself up and down, up and down. He sprang upright again and then, bending his knees, started leaping like a jack-in-a-box, looking quite ridiculous. Tom found it hard not to laugh.

"Why do we have to do these exercises, sir?" asked Susan, who'd just climbed down from the rails on the wall.

"Got to keep fit," said Mr Carstairs, who was now just a blur as he catapulted himself down to the floor and up again, endlessly. "And you don't want to seize up in the pool."

"But why do we have to keep fit?"

"Good for your health," he said, slowing down and shaking his hands in a relaxing movement. Tom thought he looked a complete prat.

"Just good for your health?" said Susan, lolling on the vaulting horse.

"Er..." Mr Carstairs looked puzzled. "Well, we've got to be fit for the Paris trip, eh? This time tomorrow we'll be walking up Montmartre, the Eiffel Tower." (Tom hoped he didn't mean *literally* walking up the Eiffel Tower. Surely they had lifts?) "We'll be hurrying to the West Bank, marching round the Louvre ... got to be fit for that, eh?"

"But I'm not going," said Susan flatly.

Mr Carstairs frowned. "Well, these exercises

are approved by the army," he said rather desperately. "Make you fighting fit."

"That's all very well for boys," said Susan. "In my book, *Rights for Kids!* it says boys can join the armed forces with their parents' consent at sixteen but girls can't join until they're seventeen and a half. It's not fair. Not that I'd want to fight."

"You should complain," said Mr Carstairs. "Take it to the race relations board. I mean sex discrimination council."

Susan brightened. "Yes, I could. Because you know you can complain if you believe you are discriminated against on the basis of race, colour, ethnic or national origin, or nationality, or on grounds of sex – whatever age you are."

"Bet you can't if you're three years old," said Miles, trying to walk on his hands (difficult when Sheila started tickling his toes just as he'd got his feet up in the air).

"You can," said Susan. "It says so in my book."

"Prove it. Ow!" he said to Sheila. "Stop that!"

"I can't. I still can't find it," said Susan, coming over and tickling his other foot till he screamed and collapsed on the floor.

"Come on now," said Mr Carstairs. "That's enough limbering up. Let's get down to the serious exercises."

Tom groaned. He already felt as if he'd run the London Marathon and there was still half the lesson to go.

As Susan lay awake that night she racked her brains to think where she might have left her book. It really bugged her to have lost it. Particularly as she wanted to have something to do when everyone else was off in Paris. She'd felt quite left out that evening, with her best friends packing their dictionaries and their cameras and yelling "Ooo-la-la" to each other across the corridor.

In her mind she went over her route the last time she'd had the book. She'd been reading it in the train ... she'd had it on the coach from the station. But she hadn't seen it again, not even when she'd unpacked. And yet she couldn't have left it on the coach because the driver always searched the seats before he went off and he would have noticed it. Unless he'd pinched it, but he would hardly want a book called *Rights for Kids!* when he was probably at least thirty.

There was only one place it might be, she remembered suddenly. As she'd got out of the coach, she'd tripped over little Arthur Mitsford – so maybe it had dropped on to the gravel or into the bushes. She'd look tomorrow. She turned over to go sleep.

But what if it rained in the night? Or what if

someone found it before her tomorrow morning? She kept arguing with herself. And when she'd decided, emphatically, that it would be ridiculous to go searching for her book in the freezing cold in the middle of the night, she just couldn't get to sleep. There was nothing for it. Crazy as it was, she had to look for the book. Cursing, she stole out of bed, careful not to wake Rosemary, and, pulling on her dressing gown and grabbing her torch, she tiptoed downstairs. The front door was locked – but there was a fire door round the back and if she wedged it open she could get back in again.

She crept down the corridor, past the deserted classrooms, through the cloakroom where a hundred raincoats hung, into the sports equipment room with its racks of hockey sticks, cricket bats and tennis rackets, and out into the garden. She looked at her watch. Midnight! This was ridiculous! Still, she'd never be able to sleep without looking.

Outside it was pitch black. She stumbled round to the front and, with her torch on, started poking through the bushes. Suddenly she glimpsed the corner of her book. Stretching into the branches, through the snow-clad leaves, she picked it up and shook it delightedly.

Great! But as she turned to sneak back, her attention was caught by a strange dark shape in the shadows.

33

She'd always been told to scream and run if any creepy strangers approached her – but instead, she froze. Who was it? Mr Fox? A mad rapist? Then the black figure stepped out of the shadows and into her path.

"Good evening," said the figure. Its voice was low and cracked as if it came from many centuries ago.

"G-good..." said Susan. But her voice dried up after that. The hairs on the back of her neck started to rise and her heart was beating rapidly. From being bitterly cold a second ago, she was terribly hot. She felt her cheeks flaming with fear.

For a while they both stood motionless. Then Susan slowly became aware of a dreadful smell – a smell of drains and death, of mould and coffins and decay.

The figure moved into the pool of light made by her torch.

It was a grotesque creature that stood before her. It was dressed in a huge black cloak and over its head – assuming it was a head – was a great black bag, with only slits for eyes. It seemed to have no hands – they were under the cloak – and it was only because it spoke and moved that you could tell it was a living creature at all. Or was it? There was something ghostly and eerie about it.

"You are not Mr Fox!" said the figure, angrily, as it got closer.

"N-no ... I'm ... er..."

The dreadful smell grew worse.

"The fool!" it said. "Surely the science block was enough! How much more do I have to do before he obeys me!" The figure twitched angrily. "Now, you! I suppose you are some wretched pupil at this school. My school!"

"Er ... y-yes..." said Susan, wondering how she could possibly run past the creature without it catching her. But its eyes, thin lines of grey light that filtered like steel through the slits in its hood, seemed to hold her immobile.

"Follow me!" The creature snapped out this command with a swirl of its black cloak. As the garment moved, it let out a great gust that smelled of dead rats; then the thing turned on its heel. Clutching her book, Susan followed.

Down the gravel path she walked, in a hypnotic trance, until it paused at a clearing near some bushes. Pushing back the leaves, the creature revealed a huge iron door which was slightly ajar. It gave a creak like a groan as it was opened; then the black shape marched firmly ahead and Susan followed, the door giving a shriek as it closed behind her.

Susan stepped into an extraordinary world. It seemed to be a vast underground cavern, with steps leading down to a pit of darkness. Ahead, the figure glided down the slimy stairs; Susan had to follow. If only she could turn back and run – but her feet wouldn't obey her orders.

As her footsteps echoed round the stairwell Susan started to make out what lay below. It seemed there was a small harbour, consisting of a slippery, black quay beside a black pond of murky water.

Down and down she stepped, not noticing the rats with glittering eyes that popped out of holes in the rock as she passed; not noticing the rocky walls dripping with putrid globules of greasy water which made splatting noises as they fell on to the rocks below – until she finally came to the quay. The creature was bending over now, pulling at a black rope that made slapping sounds as it hit the sludgy water; eventually it hauled in a small boat that looked as if it were made of rotten wood, and tied it fast. The figure stepped on board, turned, and beckoned to her. Beckoning to go – who knew where?

Powerless, Susan reached out her hand to the figure, who reached back. Its grip was terrifyingly cold and tenacious.

But just as she was about to step on to the craft, there was a splashing and snapping from the water. A vicious yellow animal, a monster with rows of serrated teeth, snapped up at her from the slime, filling her with terror. Involuntarily, she stepped back with a shriek, and at the sound of her own voice, she seemed to break the spell.

She didn't wait to look around. She scrambled back up the steps, slipping and sliding as she ran. The flight seemed about ten times longer than when she had come down but up and up she went, falling, bruising herself, stumbling up the next ten steps, and then falling back five, and then on and on and up and up till she finally came to the door. Flinging herself against it, she crashed into the shrubbery. Picking herself up and gathering her dressing gown high to give her speed, Susan raced back through the fire door and up the stairs, and eventually, gasping and crying, found herself in her own corridor. Instinctively she rushed, as quietly as she could, to Tom and Miles' room.

"Tom! Miles!" she whispered hysterically, knocking on the door. "Let me in! Help me!"

CHAPTER THREE

"What? What time is it?" Tom fumbled for the light switch and, reaching out, he pulled the door open. There stood Susan in her dressing gown, white-faced but still clutching the *Rights for Kids!* book.

Miles turned over in his sleep and groaned, rubbing his eyes. "Surely it's not time to leave for Paris yet! I've only just got to sleep," he moaned. Then, seeing Susan and her book, he said, "OK, you found it. But couldn't you have waited till morning to tell us? We've got to get up at the crack of dawn for the coach!"

Susan said nothing – just stared at them in a state of shock. "I-I'm s-sorry," she said, in a low monotone. Her eyes were two unblinking glass balls, her face was ashen and her jaw rigid, like carved wood. And her wild frizzy red hair seemed to be even wilder, redder and frizzier than usual.

Tom stared at her for a moment longer. No, there was something really wrong! He leapt up and put his arm round her.

"What's the matter?" he said kindly. "Don't worry about waking us up. What's happened?"

Miles leaned forward more anxiously, rubbing his eyes. "You look as if you've seen a ghost," he said. "Poor old thing. Have some

Coke. I've got a bit left in my bag from the journey. It's a bit flat I'm afraid." He leaned forward and rummaged round for an old plastic bottle in the bag that was on the end of his bed.

"I *have* seen a ghost!" Susan burst out suddenly. Then she started trembling.

"Shock," said Miles efficiently. "Keep her warm, that's what my dad always says." Miles' dad was a Harley Street doctor. Tom pulled the top blanket from his bed and wrapped it round Susan.

"And give the patient a cup of hot, sweet tea. Or, in this case," Miles added, handing over the bottle, "cold, flat Coca-Cola." Susan's teeth were chattering so much it took quite a while for the story to emerge. And she was stammering so with fright that it was quite difficult for Tom and Miles to understand.

"H-he was dressed in this black c-cloak," she ended up. "And he t-took me down to these underground c-c-c-c..."

"Caterpillars?" suggested Miles. "Crocuses? Car parks? Caves?"

Susan nodded. "Caves. He was going to take me in a boat but then I came to and ran away."

"It must have been a dream," said Miles. "Night terrors. You can still get them even at our age."

Susan held up her book with a shaking hand. "Then what's this?" she asked, calming

39

down a bit. "How could it have been a dream? I *did* go out and I found my book in the bushes. Then this – this *thing* appeared."

Tom looked doubtful. "Maybe you were asleep and dreamt where you'd left the book – it can happen," he said. "Then you kind of half woke, went downstairs, got it and then fell asleep again. You probably sleep-walked and had this frightening dream. And then you tripped or something, woke up and came rushing up here."

Miles agreed, nodding wisely. "Sounds like a good theory to me," he said.

Susan shook her head. "No, no, it was real. It was terrifying. Oh, I wish you two weren't going to Paris tomorrow!"

"Today, you mean," said Miles, looking at his watch.

"I'm so frightened! I'll be all on my own!"

"You'll have Rosemary, she's not going – and at least half the class as well," said Miles. "And look, when we get back we'll come with you and search the grounds for this door."

"Oh, please would you?" said Susan, her eyes lighting up. "Please, please!"

"But I bet it's not there," said Tom.

"You see, you don't believe me!" said Susan, bursting into tears. "You just think I'm a h-hysterical woman!"

Over on his bed Miles nodded his head to Tom, mouthing, "Correct!"

Tom gave Susan a hug, comforting her. "Of course we don't," he said. "We believe you believe it..."

"You believe I believe it!" snapped Susan, rubbing her eyes furiously with her hand. "What kind of patronizing remark is that!"

"No, no, I believe you," said Tom, realizing he'd never get back to sleep unless he lied. "Come on, I'll take you back to your room and make sure you're safe. You'll feel better tomorrow after a good sleep."

"OK," said Susan rather miserably. She got up, wiped her eyes on her dressing gown and smiled at Miles. "Thanks for the Coke, Miles," she said. "I'll miss you when you're gone."

"It's only two days," said Miles. "And when we get back we'll do a thorough search, I promise."

"What's tall, French and wobbles?"

The whole group was sitting in a café on the Champs-Elysées in Paris, recovering from a journey that had taken an entire day. It was cold and starting to get dark, but Miss Shepherd had insisted that they all went to the Champs-Elysées on their first night or, she had said, "it wouldn't feel like being in Paris".

Tom was glad they'd come. It was the first sensible thing Miss Shepherd had ever said. His mum and dad always insisted, whenever they went to the seaside for their holidays, that however late they arrived they had to go down to the sea and put their feet in the water just to make certain they were really there.

It was all very French. Round them waiters in long white aprons gabbled incomprehensibly, people gesticulated to each other just like they did in films, and they'd actually seen a man with a beret and a long bit of bread under his arm. There was an atmosphere, a smell about the place that was foreign and exotic. The traffic along the wide street honked and hooted; on the other side, as dusk fell, other cafés were putting on their lights. Miles made his thumb and forefinger into a little circle, put the tips of his fingers to his lips, and kissed them.

"What *is* tall, French and wobbles?" asked Sheila curiously.

"The Trifle Tower!" exclaimed Asquith Minor triumphantly. "What kind of sandwiches swing from bells?"

"Dunno," said Miles, fishing in the bottom of his glass for ice.

"*Loud* sandwiches," said Simon, giggling.

Everyone looked him crossly. "Loud sandwiches! It doesn't make sense."

"The Lunchpack of Notre Dame!" shouted Asquith Minor. "What's yellow and round and goes round and round?"

At this point Mr Carstairs came over with a clipboard.

"Now, we're all going to get something to eat in a place nearer the hostel, and then we'll go back for an early night. But tomorrow we're going to the Louvre to see the pictures and to Notre Dame and the next day it's Montmartre and the Eiffel Tower. And in the evening we're going to see a French film, as a special treat, to improve your French. It's *Phantom of the Opera* – no, it's *not* the musical, it's a different version. The old one."

"Shame!" said Simon. Sheila made a face at Sophie.

"Excellent!" said Miles as they got up to follow Mr Carstairs back towards the youth hostel. "By the way, Asquith Minor, what *is* yellow and round and goes round and round?"

"I know!" said Simon. "A ball!"

Everyone turned on him. "No, stupid," said Asquith Minor. "A long-playing omelette."

While the kids in Paris were tucking into their first-ever helping of *pommes frites* and trying one snail each from the single dish they'd ordered (in case they didn't like them), the situation at Burlap Hall was reaching crisis point.

That morning Mr Fox had called in the assessors from the Trustus Insurance Company to examine the remains of the science block. These were the people who the insurance company sent to make sure that it was a genuine accident. As Mr Cockroach and Mr Woodlouse, the two assessors, drove down the lane towards Burlap Hall, they were overtaken by three fire engines, screaming and hooting.

Smoke was pouring from what once had been the kitchen wing of Burlap Hall but which was, at this very moment, just a pile of smouldering cinders. The whole school seemed to be outside on the lawn, children huddled in blankets, small children crying, teachers looking worried as the firemen hosed down the smouldering ruins that remained. Mr Fox came rushing up to the insurance assessors' car.

"Look! Look!" he cried, pointing. "Another accident! There's a curse on this place! Get out quickly and see what the damage is! You'll have to include this on your assessment I'm afraid. Oh, pessimissimus!"

He shook his head both in horror at what was happening to his school and in fear at what he had just said. Perhaps it *was* a curse? And if it was, did the insurance policy include cover for curses? He knew that insurance policies often had tiny bits written into them in minuscule writing which meant that when you claimed the money back on something that had been damaged the insurance people all too often roared with laughter, got out a magnifying glass and pointed to the small print which always seemed to say "all money paid for accidents *except* in the case of..." and there written

44

would be exactly what your problem was.

"Curses, curses!" he muttered to himself. "I should never have mentioned curses!" Then he looked up anxiously. He should never have said that, either. Perhaps they'd heard.

Mr Carstairs came rushing up asking if there was anything he could do, and Mrs Grain said that a parent was on the phone wanting to talk to him about what was going to happen to the science classes now the science building had collapsed, and three of the smaller children had come up saying they were hungry and wanted some breakfast. Mr Fox felt like tearing his hair, but there was so little left to tear he decided against it and just clutched his head instead, moaning.

Mr Cockroach and Mr Woodlouse had already produced a variety of instruments and tape-measures and were busy taking Polaroids of the scene of the accident and making notes.

"Most extraordinary!" said Mr Cockroach. "Kitchens did you say?"

"Yes," replied Mr Fox. "But no one was there at this time. We never have cooked breakfasts at Burlap Hall. There was no gas or electricity on."

"No chip pans?" asked Mr Cockroach.

"Not at breakfast!" said Mr Fox crossly.

"I wonder," said Mr Woodlouse, "if two cornflakes could have accidentally rubbed together, then one of the bits of sugar coating

45

could have reflected the sun through the window, and started a blaze within the bowl of dry cornflakes, *before* the milk had been added?"

"If so," said Mr Cockroach, smiling, "you're not covered. Definitely not. There is some small print under clause five which specifies specifically that."

"There is no sun!" said Mr Fox triumphantly, pointing to the grey clouds above.

"Act of God?" said Mr Cockroach.

"What do you mean, 'Act of God'?" asked Mr Fox. His feet were getting cold out there and he wanted to go inside and have a stiff drink to calm himself.

"Invariably you will find that if there is no explanation at all for an accident happening, we put it down to an Act of God. Acts of God are not covered under your insurance policy," said Mr Woodlouse, checking through his files.

"If we do find a reason for this accident occurring, and if in any part it is remotely your fault or even in some – or indeed most – cases not your fault, then invariably the accident is automatically excluded from our policy," said Mr Cockroach.

"And that means you won't get the money," added Mr Woodlouse, rubbing his hands with a smile.

"I'm going in," said Mr Fox gloomily. "You look around and I'll be in my study. Then I'd better take assembly. I've got a school to run."

* * *

Susan had woken up still feeling very wobbly from her experiences the night before. She knew that Tom and Miles hadn't believed her, and now it was morning she was starting to wonder whether it hadn't been a dream after all. She went through it again in her mind. Finally, she examined her slippers, looking at the soles. They were still damp. She ran a finger over them. It picked up a streak of black slime – the sort of slime that had covered those dank steps. She sniffed. The unmistakable smell made her come out in gooseflesh; the smell of old drains and death. It was just as she put them down that Rosemary burst in, fresh from the bathroom. "Hurry up!" she said. "The kitchens are on fire! Let's go down and have a look! First the science block and now the kitchens! Whatever next! Soon there won't be anything left of the school!"

Susan felt a shiver of fear shoot through her body. In some awful way all this was connected. She knew it in her bones. The thing in the black cloak, the disasters – they were tied up together. That creepy black shape, the underground tunnels – a hammering started up in her brain and she desperately wanted to tell Rosemary about what had happened. But ... Rosemary would never believe her. Susan said nothing as she dressed and followed Rosemary downstairs. By then the fire engines were packing up and everyone was filing back into the school looking worried.

Mr Fox was beside himself. It was only because Mr Fritz had got in touch with some local caterers who would provide breakfast for the children in an hour or so – and supply some makeshift meal service until the kitchens got built again – that he hadn't gone up to his study and put a gun to his head. That was how he felt. In complete despair.

Assembly was a gloomy affair. He rearanged the strands of hair over his balding head while Signor Ruzzi sat down at his new piano, about to launch into a rousing version of the school anthem. Along with the rest of the school, Mr Fox opened his mouth to sing as Signor Ruzzi raised his hands to begin.

But Signor Ruzzi's first notes were drowned by an enormous explosion. The entire piano flew into thousands of pieces with the most awful sound of twanging and tinkling. Strings leapt out, twanging, hammers sprang out of the case like confetti, hurtling like hailstones into the crowded assembly hall. White notes, black notes flew everywhere – up to the ceiling, into the air.

Signor Ruzzi himself was hit on the nose with an E flat and Mr Fox got a G sharp smack on his bottom.

First Signor Ruzzi screamed; then he started to cry. Mr Fox gave a squeaky moan, Mr Roy fussed around with a handkerchief and Mrs Grain stood like a goldfish with her eyes wide open in horror. The whole hall hummed with a burble of consternation. Mr Woodlouse and Mr Cockroach burst into the hall from the back. Or rather, they burst in as much as insurance assessors ever burst in anywhere. In other words, they walked rather quickly.

"Another accident!" said Mr Woodlouse to Mr Cockroach.

"Or another event that might be *construed* as an accident," said Mr Cockroach to Mr Woodlouse.

"Or, more likely," said Mr Woodlouse, smiling knowingly, "an Act of God, I'll be bound!" And they both hurried up to examine the damage.

By the middle of the following day all the kids on the Paris trip were completely knackered. They'd walked and walked, seeing everything from the *Mona Lisa* to Montmartre.

Miles had wanted to go the *Folies Bergère* to see the dancing girls but Mr Carstairs had said it was too expensive and their parents wouldn't approve anyway. But both Tom and Miles noticed that he wasn't about at supper – Miss Shepherd supervised it – and it didn't take a genius, Miles had said, to work out exactly where Mr Carstairs had gone that night.

The Eiffel Tower was spectacular and Tom

used some of his spending money on a couple of tiny charms in the shape of the Eiffel Tower. He put one on a chain round his neck – the other was for Susan – but it was a bit scratchy. Then they stopped for a really yummy lunch of pancakes, or crêpes as they were called. ("What did the French ghost say when he handed round the supper?" asked Asquith Minor. "Woo-oo-oo!" said Simon. Everyone looked at him sternly. "Want to know?" said Asquith Minor. "OK. 'I'm going to give you the crêpes!'" Everyone groaned except those who didn't understand. Like Simon.)

Then it was off to their last Paris treat, *Phantom of the Opera*.

Miles and Tom didn't understand a word of what the actors were saying – but you didn't really need to. The pictures told the whole story. It was about an opera house which was taken over by new management. But it was haunted by its previous owner, an evil man who lived in caverns under the opera house. By blackmailing the owners and threatening to destroy the building unless they did what he wanted, he got his own productions staged ... until he was defeated by the hero.

"Ugh!" said Tom to Miles when they all came out. "What a creep."

"I didn't understand it," said Simon.

"You never do," said Asquith Minor.

* * *

Back at the school Mr Cockroach and Mr Woodlouse had left Mr Fox on the verge of a nervous breakdown, promising a report but unable to find any explanation for the mysterious happenings.

And as for Susan, she just couldn't concentrate on her work. All through the day she was haunted by memories of the night before. Those eyes like slits – the terrible smell – the boat – and where had he been going to take her? A horrible little voice inside her seemed to whisper, "Wouldn't you like to find out?" and it wouldn't go away. If only Tom and Miles were here! They'd go looking for the door and everything would be all right.

After supper she stumbled upstairs early. But when she'd got undressed she just sat on the bed, unable to take the decision to get in. When Rosemary eventually came up, she found Susan in her nightdress, staring into space.

"What are you up to?" she said, snapping on the light and drawing the curtains. She neatened up the row of ballet shoes against the wall.

"Nothing," said Susan. But she didn't really hear what Rosemary was saying. And as soon as Rosemary had got into bed and turned out the light, Susan put on her slippers and dressing gown. Where was she going? She didn't know. She just felt something drawing her like a magnet, something strange and sinister. She walked down the corridor towards the fire door, as if in a trance.

Someone – something – was calling her.

CHAPTER FOUR

When Tom and Miles got back to Burlap Hall, it wasn't the usual scene that awaited them at breakfast. None of the other pupils seemed comfortable. An atmosphere of fear hung in the air. Everyone seemed to be treading carefully, as if a board might give, or a bench might break. Little Arthur Mitsford was surreptitiously measuring a small crack he'd noticed on the wall the day before. "I'm sure it's got bigger," he said to his even smaller friend as they sat down. "I'm sure this dining room's going to collapse on us just as we're eating."

"Oh, don't," said his friend. "I'm frightened."

And it wasn't the usual Susan who sat between Tom and Miles eating her cornflakes, either. The usual Susan would have punched them playfully on the back and called them "guys" and winked at them and hooted with laughter about their experiences. No, Susan had changed.

She was extremely pale, wore a frown of concentration as if she were trying to memorize something and, when she was spoken to, replied with a far-away look in her eyes.

"Look, I bought this for you!" said Tom, sliding along the bench at breakfast with his cornflakes in one hand and his tea and Eiffel

Tower model in the other. He handed her the little silver charm. "I hope you like it."

Susan took it and looked at it vaguely. She turned it over as if it were a dead fly. "Ah, the Eiffel Tower," she said, in a low voice. "Built by the French engineer Alexandre Gustave Eiffel for the Paris Exhibition of 1889."

Tom did a double-take, mid-cornflakes. "What?" he said. "How did you know that?"

"The tower," replied Susan dully, "which is made of iron, is three hundred metres high and weighs about seven hundred tonnes." She put the little model on the table and stared into space.

"Well, do you like it?" asked Tom, still confused but feeling his present deserved at least a "thank you".

"Yes," replied Susan. Nothing more.

"So, what's been going on here since we were away?" asked Miles, helping himself to more milk. "I hear the kitchens burnt down – and Signor Ruzzi's piano blew up! Wish we'd been here to see that! Was he very upset?"

"Very upset," said Susan, pushing aside her unfinished bowl of cornflakes. She stared straight ahead. "The stones of Burlap Hall date back in part to the mid-seventeenth century. They will be impossible to replace. Burlap Hall itself is one of the most exceptional schools in the country, established as it was in the early 1800s and brought to its peak

54

under the Victorian headmaster, Mr Horace Squooch."

"Oh really?" said Miles, looking at her rather oddly. Behind her back he made a face at Tom while putting a finger to his temple and wiggling it to show he thought she was batty. He made an attempt to tell her about Notre Dame and Montmartre, and Tom, in a fit of desperation, tried to get a response by telling her Asquith Minor's jokes, but his stories met with the same blank stare. Except for one moment: when he got to the joke about the long-playing omelette Susan suddenly snapped back to her old self.

"Long-playing omelette!" she said, her face suddenly alive. "Honestly, you guys, I've never heard such corny jokes! I wish I'd come with you!" But then her face changed as if she'd remembered something. "No, I don't," she said. "Because then I would have missed my lessons with the..." But then she clammed up and refused to talk again, relapsing into sad concentration.

Miles tried a final tack.

"Well, we're all prepared to look for that door you told us about!" he said. "How about at break?"

But the mention of the door drew only a faint response from Susan. She turned to him, unsmiling. "There is no door," she said flatly.

"No door!" said Tom. "What's the matter

with you! Before we went you were in the most terrible state! You begged us to look for some door you said led to underground caves!"

Susan turned to him with a look of blank fury. "There is no door!" she said, her voice quivering with anger. "There are no caves! I trust this is the last time I have to suffer hearing about the subject!"

"But the dream..." blurted out Miles.

"A dream," said Susan emphatically. "Nothing but a dream. Let's hear no more on the subject."

Tom raised his eyebrows at Miles and shrugged. "OK," he said dejectedly. "Anything you want." Together he and Miles took their bowls to the stacking trolleys at the top of the hall. As Tom passed Mr Fox, he couldn't help noticing that he looked even more fraught than usual.

"Ever so sorry about the kitchens, sir," he said.

Mr Fox glanced up at him abstractedly, wiping cornflakes from his chin.

"Thank you, Roger," he said. Clearly, he was in another world. What *was* the place coming to, thought Tom.

Mr Fox's mind was on other things. For a start there had been yet another letter that morning. He could *smell* there was another letter because there was a new odour in his study, an odour that permeated the usual reek of stale smoke, dried whisky-dregs, old books and pongy slippers. Added to this interesting perfume stew, there was the very distinct smell of drains. And as he smelt it, his heart sank. Slowly he was starting to piece together a pattern. Every time he had a letter and didn't carry out the instructions, something dreadful happened.

This one brought the point home.

WILL YOU NEVER LEARN? it read. *You have one last chance. Tonight. Same time, same place. Or else.*

Yours,

The Phantom

Mr Fox actually jumped up and down when he read this. In a frenzy of rage he banged his fist on his desk, stamped his feet and, clamping a hand over his mouth so no one would hear him, screamed as loudly as he could. His heart was pounding and he started to sweat with fury and fear. Finally he yelled, "I can't stand it any more!" – and he summoned Mr Fritz from a science lesson.

"Fritz, my dear chap, have a chair," he said. "I have received this note and I'm at my wits' end. Quite honestly, I'm starting to believe that the events and the letters are connected, however unlikely it seems. But what can it all

57

mean? Can you shed any light on the subject?"

Mr Fritz sat down and studied the note. After a long while he shook his head.

"As a scientist I have to advise you that there is no logical explanation for any connection between these notes and the catastrophic events that have overtaken Burlap Hall."

Mr Fox coughed and looked nervous. He got up and shut the window behind him, then checked that the door was properly closed. Satisfied, he returned to his desk. He leant forward over the desk until his bulbous nose was almost touching Mr Fritz's face and said in a whisper, "But what about *illogical*?"

Mr Fritz gave a hearty laugh. "You mean supernatural? My dear Headmaster, the illogical and supernatural have no place in science!" But in his heart of hearts even Mr Fritz was wondering. The connection seemed so uncanny. "Look, leave it this time and let's see what happens. I'm sure this is just a set of unfortunate coincidences. But, if there's another disaster, perhaps we should think again."

"'*Leave it this time and let's see what happens!*'" Mr Fox's voice reached a squeak. His face turned red and one of his famous "Looks" started to creep over it. His eyebrows bristled like a porcupine's quills, his cheeks puffed out like a giant fish on the attack, and his ears propelled round like satellite dishes.

"What do you mean! What else *can* happen?

58

There's hardly anything left! There's only the sports centre and the school itself! The pupils are becoming panicky, and even the teachers are starting to talk. I discovered that Miss Shepherd has actually applied for a post at another school!" (He didn't admit that he often steamed open odd-looking post leaving Burlap Hall just in case there was something he needed to know.) "Can we afford to *leave it this time and let's see what happens*, Mr Fritz? That's what I want to know! Someone – " (and when he said "someone" the last person on his mind was himself) – "Someone must make this rendezvous. Someone," he added, to make his intentions absolutely clear, "with a fine, logical, scientific mind!"

Mr Fritz was startled by the strength of the response. "Well, if you feel so strongly, Headmaster, of course. I mean there can be no harm, can there? It's only a matter of getting up at midnight and going downstairs, isn't it? If it would put your mind at rest..." Mr Fox was just sighing with relief when he heard Mr Fritz add, "If I were you, yes, I would go. I think you should."

Now Mr Fox's sigh turned to an involuntary gasp. He didn't *feel* like going down at midnight to meet some strange ... well, he wasn't sure what it would turn out to be. It would be very dark, he thought, and cold. And frightening. He looked hopefully at Mr Fritz, wondering if he could screw up courage to ask him to accompany him but he couldn't. He'd look such a prat. And Mr Fritz clearly wasn't going to suggest it. He just looked back amiably.

"I think I shall take your advice," said Mr Fox finally, "and not go. You are right. Wait and see. In the mean time," he added, pompously, "we must discuss the GCSE syllabus for the top form after assembly. Be here at nine-thirty on the dot, Fritz!"

Victorian social history was the topic of Mrs Grain's lesson. So far they'd done the Church (boring), the class system (incredibly boring), and now they were just tackling education (terminally boring). Even Sheila and Rosemary, the most hard-working in the class, were sighing, and an attack of yawning seemed to have overtaken everyone as Mrs Grain held forth.

"In the nineteenth century," she started (why was it that any sentence starting "in the somethingth century" was always so dull?), "there was very little education. The upper classes employed governesses who lived with the family; working class children received no education at all."

"Were there any boarding schools?" asked Simon, who'd been told that if he didn't pay more attention in future he'd be sent to see Mr Fox. The result was an endless flow of inane questions.

"There were some, and some were very good," said Mrs Grain patting her neat bun. "But there were a lot of schools that were not very good, and some that were downright cruel."

"Like Burlap Hall," whispered Miles to Tom.

"Why cruel?" asked Simon.

"Parents sent children to these so-called Yorkshire schools – because most of them were in Yorkshire, far away from the prying eyes of London. And frequently the children there were put to work and not taught anything. Often there weren't even any holidays. They weren't properly fed and were very badly treated and sometimes they died."

"Why?" asked Simon, staring out of the window.

"Because they were badly treated and not given enough to eat," said Mrs Grain, irritated.

"Why?" asked Simon, flicking a pellet of paper across his desk.

"Because the headmasters were just out to make money and didn't care about the children," said Mrs Grain. "Could you put that piece of paper away, Simon? I sometimes know what those headmasters felt like when confronted with children!"

Susan's hand shot up. "All this changed, of course, with the ridiculous Education Act of 1870 when it was ordered that a school should be placed within the reach of every English child."

There was a stunned gasp from all the children as they listened to Susan talking. They had never heard anything like it. Even Mrs Grain rubbed her eyes. "Excuse me!" she said. "How did you know this? And why do you describe one of the greatest educational reforms in history as ridiculous?"

Susan continued, "This was followed in 1877 by another extremely foolish act, the Universities of Oxford and Cambridge Act, the main effect being to give the two universities a clearer footing as distinct from their constituent colleges, to render the endowments of the latter more freely available for purposes of learning, and so to open doors for widening and modernizing curricula."

You could have heard a pin drop.

"Yer wha..." whispered Tom, astonished by this display of knowledge.

But it was Simon who broke the silence.

"Why?" he asked.

At lunch Susan sat on her own. She didn't want anyone else near her. She didn't understand what was happening to her and even though she wanted to speak about it, she couldn't. Her mind was just filled with facts, facts and more facts, as if it were a camera that had taken photographs of hundreds of books and encyclopaedias. Just occasionally she would have a memory – a boat made of rotten dark wood, a grip on her wrist, the *slap, slap* of water against the side of the boat and glittering eyes, peering from two slits in a black hood.

The smell was the worst, the sickening smell of drains as the journey continued, through underground caverns and canals, past great dripping chambers of rocks and slime, on and on, with the black-cloaked figure sitting opposite, rowing the boat silently and staring into her eyes. Then they'd come to a final cavern, a cavern lined with books, and her hand would be taken again and together they'd sit down and read. Facts, facts, more facts. Everything stuffed into her head. Only occasionally was there praise.

A soft: "My star pupil! My own creation!" before more information was delivered, crammed into her head by some mysterious process she couldn't understand. Then, when her head was aching, she would be led back to the boat, they would make the return journey, and the creature would leave her at the bottom of the slimy steps with the same words, always the same words: "Until tomorrow, my dear. And not a word of this – on pain of death!"

Sometimes flashes of her old life would pop through the fact-filled room that was now Susan's brain, flashes like glimpsed views from a dark train. As she automatically put her dishes away in the large metal trolleys that lined the dining hall, she saw Tom and Miles getting up on the other side of the room. If only she could speak to them! They were her best friends, after all. But every time she tried she found she couldn't communicate. It was as if an invisible hand covered her mouth. Feeling very lonely, she went out and made her way to the library where she opened a large book and continued her compulsive studying.

As for Tom and Miles, they were baffled by Susan's recent behaviour in class. They didn't have a chance to discuss it until their afternoon run with Mr Carstairs. Today they had to run over the lawn, down through the woods, over the stream where the now-melting snow had swollen its banks, down past the spinney and up to the villages. Mr Carstairs was timing them with a stop-watch. "Give it all you've got, lads!" he yelled. "And ladesses – I mean ladies! I mean girls! Get the ground burning under your feet!"

"Fine chance in this weather," said Miles, casting a gloomy look at the cold grey skies as his feet crunched on the frosty ground beneath.

"So what do you make of Susan?" asked Tom as they panted to the end of the lawn.

"Weird," said Miles, slowing down once they were in the wood, out of Mr Carstairs' view. Past them shot Simon, then Rosemary and then Asquith Minor, followed by a crowd of other children running and cheering. "Do you think she was doing extra work when we were away?"

"It's more than extra work," said Tom. "It's a whole new language. She sounds more like a teacher than a pupil."

Miles shook his head. "Hey," he said, as they puffed through the undergrowth, trampling on frozen brambles and icy nettles. "Isn't this where Susan said that door was? Somewhere in here?"

"That's right!" said Tom excitedly, slowing down. "Let's have a look. We can always cut through to the road and miss out the spinney. No one will know."

Together they searched in the fast-fading light. They tore aside strands of ivy, pulled bushes from worn, old tree-trunks, wrenched dripping branches away from mossy knolls. But there was no sign of a door. As they got further and further into the wood it seemed to get darker and darker.

"Funny smell around here," said Tom, sniffing as he padded through the undergrowth. A bird fluttered up with a screaming sound, startling him. "Isn't there?"

There was no reply. Looking through the densely-planted trees Tom realized he had lost Miles completely. He started to panic. "Miles?" he called. "Where are you?"

There was no reply. In the greyness there was no sound at all except for the odd rustling of a leaf underfoot, expanding and contracting with changes in temperature. But there was a terrible smell of – what was it? Tom sniffed again. Drains! That was what it was. The smell was getting worse, too. He put his hand to his face to stop himself choking and as he blundered forward he fell against what seemed to be a hard rock.

Pulling away the vines and leaves that covered it, Tom gasped. Because there, in front of him, was a huge iron door, just like the one Susan had described! It was a mighty, heavy piece of metal, marked with strange letters and patterns. Down one side oozed a line of greenish slime.

"Miles! Miles!"

For a moment Tom considered trying to open it himself. Pushing against it, he opened it a crack and peeped through. But he could see nothing. And he was almost knocked over by the smell which came rushing out at him like poison gas. Falling backwards, Tom reeled, gasping for air.

He certainly wasn't going to try again on his own. If only he hadn't lost Miles, they could have tackled it together. Staring around, he tried to take in the scene so he could remember where he was; then hearing, with relief, the distant sound of a car, he started off in the direction of the road.

He got back to Burlap Hall to meet a very grim-faced Mr Carstairs, angrily staring at his stop-watch.

"An hour it's taken you! When everyone else was back forty minutes ago! Where on earth have you been? I suppose you stopped off in the village to scoff some grub!"

Tom gaped at him. He had no idea what he meant.

"You went and sneaked some chocolate from the shop! I know!" said Mr Carstairs.

"I got lost," said Tom. "Really, sir. I got to the wood, and then it started to get dark, and I only managed to get back because I heard a car on the road. It was ever so creepy out there, sir. Is Miles here? We were together and I lost him."

There must have been some genuine fear in his voice because Mr Carstairs gave him a long, hard look and eventually said, "Miles got back ages ago. Next time, stick with the others, right?"

Tom nodded and went off to change.

"I saw it, I saw it!" Tom rushed into the dining room to tell Miles. He grabbed what was left over from tea. Most of the other kids were leaving, and only a few were still at the tables finishing their bread and butter and jam.

"Saw what?" said Miles. "Phew! Where have you been? You really pong!"

"The door!" whispered Tom, scrambling on to the bench with a plate of biscuits and mug of tea. "It's there, just as Susan said!"

"Could you find it again?" asked Miles excitedly.

"I think so," said Tom, between mouthfuls and gulps. "But I can't be sure. There was such a funny smell there, too. I was scared to open it by myself."

"We can't go tonight because it's too dark. But next chance we get, let's go and explore it," said Miles, his eyes glistening. "Tomorrow in the day, eh?"

"Right," said Tom.

That night in her room, Susan found it impossible to sleep. Her mind was filled with strange bits of information. Her brain was a jumble. Sometimes she felt just like her old self; then suddenly her mind would be a whirring mass of facts and figures. And throughout all this was the image of that thing, that thing in a black hood, a thing that had a strong smell...

Almost against her will she found herself getting out of bed, silently slipping on her dressing gown and going down the hall and out into the darkness for her regular encounter with ... the thing.

* * *

The cold weather seemed to have brought out the worst in Mr Carstairs. Instead of concentrating more on the teaching of English in the warm classrooms, Carstairs, being a physical sort of chap, seemed galvanized by the icy temperatures to redouble his sporting activities. There was nothing he liked better than zooming out for a crisp run in the snow. Icy outside? All the more reason for stripping off and plunging into a swimming pool. Pouring with rain? Do some press-ups until the sun comes out.

If the truth be told, it was not just the cold weather that had this effect on Mr Carstairs. It was the presence of the refurbished sports centre which, ever since it had been built last term, had fascinated him. After the science block, it was the second pride and joy of Burlap Hall – and now, sadly, the first. There was a squash court and a room for table tennis, and a large swimming pool equipped with gleaming diving boards. Rows of seats lined the sides so parents could watch swimming events in comfort on sports day. And with this sports centre Mr Carstairs was like a child with a new toy train-set. He just couldn't keep away.

That was why he had initiated in this, the coldest of terms, the weekly early morning swim for each class.

Today was the fourth form's turn and saw a dismal queue of kids in dressing gowns over their swimming gear, waiting in the hall with their day clothes and towels rolled up in depressing little tubes under their arms. Everyone hated it – except, of course, Rosemary, who was always in such peak condition that she would happily have spent days running on the spot. True, it was nice afterwards. But then, as Miles said, after stopping anything perfectly horrible you always felt a bit better. The only thing in its favour, for Miles, was seeing Susan in a swimsuit, though this term she'd brought one that seemed to have a small skirt attached to it, which, much to Miles' disappointment, she said was the latest fashion from Paris.

That morning, Mr Carstairs was ready in the hall, running on the spot with a whistle in his mouth. "Off we go, one two, one two!" he said cheerfully. And off shambled Form Four, a reluctant mamba line following him out into the cold and into the new sports centre.

At least it was warm there, even though the atmosphere was gloomy. The swimming pool room hummed with giant boilers and stank of chlorine. The air was hot and steamy and one's voice resounded off the walls.

"A dive and five lengths, everyone!" shouted Mr Carstairs, racing up the steps of the diving board to be first in. Rosemary followed with an elegant swoop; Susan had to be reminded to go up the steps because she was lost in thought; Asquith Minor managed a belly flop, and Simon simply stood on the end, jumping up and down holding his nose, before jumping in feet first. Mr Carstairs made him try again.

Miles was always last because he insisted on watching all the girls, and Tom waited with him, hopping on the side with the wet floor cold under his bare feet.

Tom and Miles were the last two left. Tom plodded up the steps, put his hands together, and dived in first. His head broke the water's surface and down he went – and suddenly he felt a bump. As he rose to the surface, he rubbed his scalp. Could it be that his head had actually grazed the bottom of the pool? Surely not. He clambered out and sat on the side, waiting for Miles to dive. But he noticed something peculiar when he swung his feet on the edge? Something was wrong. That was it – his feet didn't touch the water. Staring hard he suddenly saw what was happening. The water was going down – and down – and down.

He could see a faint line across the floor of the swimming pool, and as he gazed, transfixed, the line grew wider and wider, revealing itself as an almighty crack in the floor.

Miles! The water was now down to about a metre deep. If Miles dived in, he'd die! Tom looked up at his friend who was bouncing on the end of the diving board preparing to leap

71

off, and screamed as loudly as he could. But Miles seemed not to hear. Mr Carstairs was talking to Asquith Minor and Miles just continued jumping up and down on the diving board.

"Miles! Miles!" screamed Tom with all his might, as the water fell lower and lower. It must be only half a metre now. No one could survive diving into water that shallow! "Don't jump! You'll be killed!"

Tom's voice seemed to get sucked into the general humming of the boilers. No one heard. Mr Carstairs continued talking, Miles simply smiled down from the diving board. The time seemed to go very slowly and what must have been only a few seconds felt to Tom like an age.

In a final attempt he screamed at the top of his voice, "MILES – DON'T JUMP!" just at the very moment that Miles, hands together, sprang off the board.

CHAPTER FIVE

But as Miles was jumping upwards he heard what Tom was yelling and glanced downwards. His eyes bulged as he saw the crack below. And with a superhuman effort he managed to twist his body round, reaching out his arms to try to catch the end of the diving board as he fell. He managed to grab it with one hand – and clung for dear life. But his fingers were slowly slipping from the wet surface.

The combined screams of Tom and Miles finally attracted Mr Carstairs, who suddenly leapt into action, raced up the diving-board steps, and, with only seconds to spare, sprang to the end to help Miles up.

The crack in the swimming pool split wide open and, with a crumbling, groaning sound, the walls of the pool caved in. Tom managed to scramble from the edge just in time to see Mr Carstairs carrying Miles, who seemed to have fainted. Above them, the diving board rocked precariously. Then, as they all rushed outside into the cold, the entire sports centre collapsed into the ground with an enormous crash.

"Oh, my giddy aunt! My goodness! Oh no, oh no!" wailed Mr Carstairs. "We might have been killed!"

"Oh, Tom, oh, sir!" said Miles, slowly coming round from his faint and putting his feet on the ground.

"Oh, sir, sir!" said Tom, on the verge of tears, clinging to the sports master's hand. It didn't seem to matter how they behaved since they were all so shocked and upset. Everything was absolutely awful.

Mr Carstairs recovered first. "If it hadn't been for you, Tom, Miles would have been killed," he said, in a rather croaky voice.

"If you hadn't been so fit, sir, you'd never have saved Miles from the diving board," said Tom. "I'll never complain about doing those exercises again."

Miles just gave a shiver. "I don't even want to think about it," he said.

Other kids, having heard the noise, had come running up, wiping bits of breakfast from their mouths, gawping at the smoking ruin that had been the sports centre. Taking up the rear was Mr Fox.

"I just can't believe it!" he said, in a strangled voice. All his blood vessels seemed to have combined in preparation for a mass explosion. Mr Fox had the feeling that he might actually spontaneously combust. It was only, he felt, because it was so cold outside that he was saved. "Oh pessimissimus, what have I done to deserve this!"

As the shivering survivors were led away to

have hot baths and cups of tea, Mr Fritz came running to the scene. He surveyed it with alarm and then turned to the headmaster.

"So – er – you didn't keep your assignation last night?" he said. It was obvious.

"I did not!" snapped Mr Fox. "I took your advice and look what happens! I hold you entirely responsible. There is definitely a connection between the letters and the disasters. I just hope I don't get another letter. But if I do I'll have to meet whoever-it-is. And see what whoever-it-is wants. In the meantime I will have to contact Earwig and Buzzard or whatever their names are. Again!"

Later that day, Tom and Miles were the heroes of the common room. A fascinated group of children of all ages crowded around them, longing to hear the story again and again. "But how did you manage to turn in mid-air?" and "Would you have been dead, really dead, completely squashed, if Tom hadn't called out?" and "Tell us again about Mr Carstairs running up the diving board!" and "How long was it after you got out that the sports centre fell down? Was it a few minutes? Or was it the very moment you got out? Did you escape *by the skin of your teeth*?"

Even Simon was asking intelligent questions and Asquith Minor was transfixed. You could see that he wished he'd been the centre of attention and had been saved by the skin of his teeth himself.

The only person who sat apart was Susan, looking extremely depressed, leafing over the pages of a history book. When all the kids grew bored with asking questions, Tom wandered up to her.

"Did you hear what happened?" he asked, rather accusingly, because he thought she, as their best friend, might have been a bit more interested in the fact that Miles had escaped death by only a whisker.

Susan looked up, her face ashen. "Yes," she said, in a low voice. "It was terrible," she said. "You and Miles might have died."

Tom nodded. "Still, we're here."

Suddenly Susan shuddered. "Oh, I'm sure it's his fault! I wish I could stop him!" she suddenly burst out, clutching Tom's hand.

"Who?" asked Tom. "What are you talking about? Do you know who's responsible for all these catastrophes?"

Susan looked at her feet. "I wish I could tell you. I can't. I don't even know what I'm talking about. I'm so frightened."

"There's nothing to be frightened of," said Tom, putting his arm round her. "What's the matter?"

But then a far-away look came into her eyes. "Nothing," she said, in a voice as dead as the slates on a roof. "Sorry. Nothing."

Tom couldn't say anything to make her budge. It was as if she'd changed into a completely different person. She started muttering to herself and as Tom listened he was astonished to hear her repeating dates: "Napoleonic War 1803-1815. 1805 – Napoleon defeated at Trafalgar. 1806 – Death of Pitt and the end of the Holy Roman Empire. 1808 – Napoleon secures all Europe except Britain, Russia and Portugal. Peninsular War – 1808-1814 led to French defeats at Vittoria, 1815, Orthez and Toulouse in 1814. His Russian campaign in 1812 ended in the retreat from Moscow. 1815, Battle of Waterloo, French defeated by Wellington."

Then she started all over again.

Meanwhile, Miles was basking in his escapee's glory with an expansive grin on his face. "Yes, it's true," he was saying to no one in particular. "I turned in mid-air. It took all the strength I had but I managed it. Heavens knows where the strength came from. But it came. The next thing I knew..."

"Miles!" said Tom, overhearing and giving him a shake. "It's me, Tom!"

"Oh, sorry," said Miles, giving a sheepish grin. "Can't stop!"

"Go and see Susan," said Tom. "There's something wrong with her. She told me she was frightened of someone, someone who sounds responsible for all these horrible disasters. Then she went all silent and now she's just reciting these dates. She's still doing it."

Standing behind Susan's chair, Miles listened as the information poured forth. "Cadmium is a metallic element, symbol Cd, chemically similar to zinc and mercury. Used in alloys to lower the melting point, as in Wood's metal with bismuth and tin. Alloyed with copper to make..."

He returned looking puzzled and anxious. "That's not like Susan," he said. "What's going on?"

Tom shook his head. "I'm convinced that door she talked about holds the answer. Let's go and look tonight. I know," he said, looking at Miles' face. "I don't want to go at night either. But when else can we go? We'll be missed if we go in the day. And anyway," he added, grinning, "you're the guy who can turn in mid-air. You're not afraid of anything."

Miles gave him a friendly kick and as the bell rang they went off to tea.

There was no point in setting off too early in case they met Mr Fox prowling around. But try as they might, it was impossible to get to sleep before the alarm went off at midnight. The fact that they had kept their clothes on made sleeping even more difficult. Tom felt funny trying to sleep with his tie on. He needed the soft rustle of his pyjamas to get him off to the land of Nod, and his school suit felt shiny and scratchy under the bedclothes.

So at midnight they rose, tiptoed down the back stairs and were just about to open the fire door when Miles said, "Sssh! I can hear something!"

They pressed themselves against a wall and listened. But it was nothing more than Form Two having a midnight pillow fight. From the floor above came muffled screams and giggles.

Tom breathed a sigh of relief and was just about to walk on when Miles held him back. "No – there's something else," he said. They both shrank into the shadows. This time there was definitely someone on the stairs and as they squeezed themselves against shelves of uncomfortable old lacrosse sticks and cricket pads, they saw a small figure coming towards the fire door. It was a girl in a dressing gown – and the walk was familiar, even in the darkness. And when she opened the door and the moonlight fell on a shivering heap of frizzy red hair, both Miles and Tom whispered simultaneously, "Susan!"

"Quick! We must follow her!" said Miles. Together they crept stealthily through the door, across the lawn and down to the woods.

It was difficult to keep up with her in the dark; Susan seemed to know exactly where she was going and hurried ahead like one following a distant call. If only she didn't hear their footsteps behind her. They plunged past trailing vines, through dank ferns and freezing piles of leaves. The tip of Tom's nose and his ears were just beginning to ache with cold when, deep in the middle of the wood, Susan disappeared.

"Is this it?" asked Miles.

Tom looked around. Even though his eyes had accustomed themselves somewhat to the dark, he couldn't really remember where the door had been. But gradually he saw what seemed to be a familiar clearing.

"Over there!" he said, pointing, and together they forged ahead until they came to the same slab of rock which Tom had crashed into on his run.

"This is the place!" said Tom. "What a pong!" Only he said "pog" instead of "pong" because he was holding his nose so he couldn't smell the odour of drains.

"The sbell!" said Miles.

"Pardod?" said Tom.

Miles shook his head and pointed to the door, gesticulating. Tom nodded and slowly, using all their strength, they pushed against it and stepped inside.

"By gooddess!" breathed Tom. Miles was speechless. Because neither of them had ever seen anything like what lay before them.

The underground cavern was huge, lit by a silvery glow that bounced off rocks glistening with slime. In the crevices, toads stared at them with yellow eyes, and small bats and night-birds flew about making a whirring noise with their wings. Below them a flight of steps, thick with moss, stretched downwards, and they could just see Susan's figure disappearing into the darkness below.

"Come on!" said Tom.

Gingerly, they stepped down and down until they reached a small platform. Another smaller flight of steps led from there to a quay. And on the quay they could see Susan, waiting. Miles was about to call her but Tom put his finger to his lips. He'd heard something. Sure enough, after only a few moments, what had been a distant splashing noise got closer and closer until a boat pulled up. And in this boat was a terrible figure cloaked in black, hunched over two ancient barnacle-covered oars. As the boat drew up to the quay, the figure rose and held out a long black-gloved hand to Susan.

"More education, my dear." It had a low, gravelly voice. "Soon you will become the cleverest student at Burlap Hall! My star pupil!"

And, taking its hand, Susan stepped on board and sat down; the black creature then rowed the boat off into the distance. The faint *slap slap* of the oars became fainter and fainter, leaving the two boys goggling in the darkness.

"Who the hell," said Tom, "was that?"

"*What* was it," said Miles. "It hardly looked human!"

"Let's go down and have a look," said Tom. "We must investigate."

Together they walked nervously down the stairs and looked around. But there was nowhere to go. Without a boat they couldn't go anywhere – unless they were prepared to swim – and neither Tom nor Miles felt like braving the soupy water that lapped at their feet. It was all rather a let-down.

"Wait for her to come back?" said Miles. "Or go back?" He said the words "Or go back" rather louder and quicker and more positively than the first part of his sentence. He certainly didn't want to stay.

"Go back," said Tom, feeling a bit of a coward. "Clearly she's met this ... this whateveritis ... before. And she's come back before. So there's nothing we can do. But what we've seen certainly explains a lot."

"Does it?" said Miles as they climbed up the steps. "I think it just makes things even more confusing."

The problem was whether or not to tell Susan they'd followed her.

"She'll only deny it," said Miles, as they ducked flying soaps and sponges in the communal bathrooms. "Lay off, Asquith Minor!" he yelled as he avoided a passing loofah. "You could kill someone with one of those!"

"Wasn't me, it was Simon," said Asquith Minor. Simon wrapped himself completely in an enormous bath-towel till only his eyes were showing. "Simon has disappeared," he announced. "I am the invisible man."

"It'd be interesting to see her reaction, though," said Tom, rubbing his hair with a towel. "Let's give it a go."

But Miles was right. Susan refused to talk about what had happened the night before. True, she'd looked very alarmed and surprised when Tom and Miles told her they'd followed her, but soon slumped back into a non-communicative state. "It was a dream you had," she said flatly.

"But two people can't have the same dream," said Tom.

"Well, you two did," said Susan. Then she went back to muttering anxiously. "Jainism. The Jains are a small Indian sect, largely in commerce and finance, numbering about two million. Their movement, founded by Vard-hamana, called mahavira (the great hero) in the sixth century BC, arose rather earlier than Buddhism in revolt against the ritualism and impersonality of Hinduism."

Tom shook his head. "We've got to talk to someone about this," he said quietly to Miles. "She's very confused."

"Mr Fritz," said Miles. "He's the only

83

teacher who has any sense round here. Come on, there's still ten minutes before lessons. Let's try to catch him now."

Mr Fritz was in the common room, hovering on the edge of a group of teachers who were all in heated discussion. From the door Tom and Miles could hear snippets of conversation. "Not good enough," Mrs Grain was saying. "Burlap Hall is turning into a bomb-site."

Mr Roy was shaking his head vigorously. "And these caterers have no idea about vegetarian diet. After all, I can't live on omelettes. And I'll swear that onion soup they gave us the other day had a beef stock cube in it. I could taste it!"

"We were once a greata schoola!" wailed Signor Ruzzi. "Roost of the cock! And now we are nothing. Heap of the bottom!"

Miss Shepherd's eyes filled with tears. "I used to *love* teaching here. Craft, cookery – but without kitchens how can one teach the art of cooking? One might as well try to teach the piano on a plank of wood!"

Mr Carstairs looked stern. "We must do something about all this. We can't go on. I shall organize a petition."

Mr Fritz was keeping out of the general conversation, but on seeing Tom and Miles peering rather mournfully round the door he extricated himself.

"Want to talk to me?" he said, tapping his pipe on the door frame. "I know the whole school is upset. Lots of the children have wanted a quiet word. They're genuinely frightened. And quite frankly, I don't blame them. It's scary when you don't know whether the roof's going to cave in on your head or not, isn't it? Let's go upstairs to my study."

Mr Fritz's study was in a worse mess than usual. Privately, Miles and Tom thought that since the science block had collapsed, Mr Fritz was actually performing experiments in his room, and certainly it looked as if he'd let off a bomb in it that morning. Clothes, books, papers were everywhere and, looking up, Tom noticed faint greenish smoke clinging to the ceiling. Mr Fritz put on a kettle for a cup of tea, hoping he hadn't put any chemicals in it by mistake.

"I can't make head or tail of these disasters myself, you know," said the science teacher. "They don't follow the laws of statistics. One disaster, two, three, maybe, but four ... no, it won't wash. There has to be some explanation."

"It wasn't really about the disasters that we came to talk to you," said Miles, rather nervously.

"Oh, a science problem?" said Mr Fritz. "Or perhaps," he said, going bright red, "the, er, facts of life?"

"No, no," said Tom hastily. "We know all about the facts of life. No, it's Susan."

Mr Fritz looked so relieved you could practically see the anxiety escaping from him like air out of a balloon.

"Ah, Susan. She's a clever girl. Even cleverer than usual, this term, I think. It's amazing what she knows."

"Well, this is what we wanted to talk to you about."

Mr Fritz leaned forward, nodding wisely. "If you want to be as clever as Susan there's only one thing for it. Work, work and more work. There are no short cuts."

Tom sighed. "No, sir," he said. And he explained the whole story about Susan's experiences and her odd behaviour and what they'd seen the night before.

Mr Fritz looked more and more interested. The bell went for the first lesson and Tom and Miles looked at each other, scrambling up, but Mr Fritz gestured for them to sit down.

"No, no. Don't go. This is far more important," he said, drawing on his pipe with a faraway look in his eyes. "I'll make your excuses. Well, what a story! I wonder if this relates in any way," he added as if to himself, "to the Phantom?"

"The Phantom!" said Tom and Miles together.

"Hush!" said Mr Fritz nervously. "I should never have mentioned it. Please, erase what I said from your minds. I was most indiscreet."

"I can't erase it from my mind. It's in there now," said Tom, rather crossly. "What's all this about the Phantom?"

"The disasters, the letters ... and now this!"

"What letters?" said Tom.

Mr Fritz sighed and tapped out his pipe. "Well, I'll tell you, but you'll have to promise me that what I say will go no further. This is just between us three, right?"

"Right."

And he told them all about the letters Mr Fox had been getting and how the disasters seemed to have followed the letters.

And suddenly everything fell into place in Tom's mind. He jumped up, breathless with excitement. "The Phantom of Burlap Hall!" he shouted.

"Sssh!" Both Miles and Mr Fritz were afraid that someone might hear.

"What do you mean, the Phantom of Burlap Hall?" added Mr Fritz.

"Don't you remember, Miles? In Paris. We saw that film. *Phantom of the Opera*. He wrote letters to the new opera managers demanding they do things his way ... or he'd wreak havoc on the place. Just like here! And there was a girl in it, too – just like Susan. He hypnotized her to make her a star!"

Mr Fritz's eyes glittered. "Yes, yes! I know the story," he said. "But who is this Phantom? And why has he only appeared now? After all, Mr Fox has been here for years."

"Perhaps he's someone who used to own Burlap Hall. An old squire. I don't know. And no," said Tom lamely, "I don't know why he would suddenly appear now."

"But still, it holds water, this idea, doesn't it?" said Miles. "If only we knew the history of Burlap Hall. Then I'm sure we could get to the bottom of it."

"Exactly!" said Mr Fritz. "I tell you what. This weekend I'll go off to London to the British Library and do some research. If I don't get to the bottom of this, my name's not Jack Robinson!"

"Your name isn't Jack Robinson," said Tom.

"Well spotted!" cried Mr Fritz. "Just testing! Now I'll write you a note to explain your absence from class and I'll catch the afternoon train. I feel we're near the solution to this mystery. I feel it in my bones!"

It was a cold crisp day when Mr Fritz arrived at the British Library. Before going inside he stared up at the great stone columns at the top of a vast row of stone steps. It was an awesome building. Somewhere in there, perhaps, lurked the secret of the Phantom of Burlap Hall.

He crossed his fingers as he climbed the steps.

Once inside the Reading Room, he asked a librarian how he might find the information he wanted. The librarian pointed wearily at a huge black noticeboard on which was written "Anatomy to Madness – left. Numbskulls to Zebras – right."

"Could be under Schools," he said, wearily. "Or you could try Phantoms."

"So – er – Phantoms – um – which way?" The librarian looked at Mr Fritz as if he were a half-wit, and pointed to the right. "You'll find it under Supernatural," he croaked.

Mr Fritz walked down a very long dark corridor, past more signs until he finally came to another board which read "Sambas – Science – Siberia – Supernatural" on the one side and "Tapdancing – Thought – Time – Toes" on the other. Each had an arrow pointing in a different direction. Mr Fritz followed the sign to Supernatural until he found yet another list: "Elves – Fairies – Ghosts – Hobgoblins – Houses of Horror – Magic – Phantoms – Poltergeists – Vampires – Werewolves – Witches – Wizards – Zombies."

Sighing, he followed the correct path, past vast arrays of dusty tomes, until he felt he must be right in the very centre of the library. And eventually he came to a door labelled "Phantoms".

There was no one around when he walked in. Cobwebs hung from the ceiling, spiders dangled from the bookshelves. A mouse even peeped at him from behind a book called *Phantom – Myth or Mystery?* and scuttled away. Mr Fritz approached the shelves nervously and finally selected three books. Staggering under their weight, he put them down on a table in the centre of the room. Then sweeping the table and chair of dust that flew off in clouds, he sat down and prepared for a long day's research.

CHAPTER SIX

"I really think, Susan," Mr Roy was saying, "that you should consider taking your GCSEs a year earlier than the others. You have come forward this term with such leaps and bounds – and we don't want to hold you back."

Susan had not replied to the geography teacher; she had just stared at him through pale, tired eyes and nodded her head.

Was it lack of sleep that was making her feel like this? Her head whirled with facts and figures all intermingled with dreams that were so strange that she was starting to wonder whether they really were dreams after all. If only she could get back to how she used to feel. Happy, giggly, fed up, gloomy, bored, full of beans – in other words, normal.

She did feel normal sometimes. But only sometimes. And even the sometimes were getting fewer and further between. But each time she felt it, she always hoped that at last her troubles would be over – and then just as she thought she was OK, she'd fall into another curious mood, compelled to go and learn and learn and learn.

But in the common room at break that day, Tom and Miles found the Susan they used to know.

"Hey, guys," she said when they came in.

(Susan was one of those Americans who called everyone "guys" even if they were girls.) "What's happening?"

Tom sat down beside her. "Not a lot," he said. "But hasn't enough happened already? If the school keeps falling down at the present rate, we'll end up having all our lessons in a tent on the lawn."

Sheila, who was sitting near by, looked up anxiously. "Do you really think so?" she said. "I'm too frightened to go to sleep sometimes, in case my bedroom collapses around me. I wish they'd find out what was wrong."

"Oh no, I was only joking," said Tom reassuringly. But he wasn't joking at all.

Miles was talking to Susan. "But at the rate you're going, you won't need any lessons, either in a classroom or a tent."

Susan looked rather embarrassed and blushed. "I don't really know what's going on," she said finally, after a long silence, and in a very low voice so Sheila wouldn't hear. "It's a bit creepy. Sometimes I think something's happening to me in my dreams."

"No, it's like we said," said Miles. "Each night you..."

Tom interrupted, giving Miles a surreptitious kick. "Each night you obviously have a dream that you're being taught all this information and then when you wake up, you're cleverer! I wish I could have dreams like that."

92

"It'd be a bit boring," said Miles. "I mean you have lessons all day, and then to go to bed and dream about them all over again – ugh! I'd rather dream about – ooh, sunlit beaches, palm trees, luscious girls..."

"Oh, Miles!" said Susan disapprovingly. "Do you think of nothing else?"

"I'm just a healthy male," said Miles defensively, flexing his muscles. "There's no harm in that."

"I bet Mr Carstairs doesn't have dreams like that. Or Mr Fox – oh, well, maybe he does. But Mr Roy wouldn't. And Mr Fritz certainly wouldn't. By the way, where is Mr Fritz?" asked Susan. "I wanted him to explain calculus to me again and someone said he'd gone to London."

"That's right," said Miles, charging ahead before Tom could stop him. "He's gone to London to find out some history about Burlap Hall to see if he can't catch this Phantom!"

Susan went completely white and Miles stopped in his tracks.

"Phantom?" she said distantly. "Phantom? Is that what they call him?" She started to tremble and then put out a hand to touch Tom's arm. "Please, both of you, do me a favour?"

Both Tom and Miles nodded, mystified.

"Don't tell me anything else. It makes me feel funny. And if I know too much ... then ... he will get it out of me somehow. And I mustn't ... no, I mustn't. Oh, what am I talking about? I don't even understand myself."

"What do you mean?" asked Tom. "Who is 'he'?"

But Susan had clammed up again. She started trembling, nervously. Then, "Oh no!" she suddenly whispered, as if she'd forgotten something. She jumped up. "I promised I'd read em-two-oh!"

"What's em-two-oh?" asked Tom.

"The encyclopaedia. The letter M to the letter O. I must go to the library. I'm sorry. See you!" And with that, she jumped up and rushed off, leaving Tom and Miles shaking their heads.

"I just hope Mr Fritz finds something," said Tom anxiously. "At this rate Susan will have a nervous breakdown. Fancy feeling you've got to read the encyclopaedia from cover to cover. Poor girl!"

Miles agreed. "And fancy dreaming about education instead of beautiful girls," he said.

"I don't think Susan would want to dream about beautiful girls," said Tom. "She'd be more likely to dream of great hunks of man-hood."

Miles nodded. "Like us," he said, giving Tom a nudge that nearly knocked him off his chair.

But in London Mr Fritz was having very little luck. As six o'clock struck he was no nearer to solving the mystery than he had been at ten that morning. He'd read about phantoms in films, phantoms in stories, real-life phantoms, photographs of phantoms, paintings of phantoms, phantoms in Russia, phantoms in China, recordings of phantoms, lesser-spotted phantoms, phantom pregnancies, big phan-toms, little phantoms and even a day in the life of a phantom. But at the end of all that work – nothing.

With a sigh Mr Fritz got up, brushing off the book-dust that clung to his hairy suit. He looked at the great pile of books that lay on the table where he'd read them and, one by one, lifted them back on to the shelves. It was so depressing to have reached a dead-end.

What he really needed, he decided, was a kipper and an early night. Then he would come back the next morning and start on Schools.

The next day was brighter, the sun was shining crisply, and inside the British Library the Schools section wasn't nearly as gloomy as the Phantoms section. There were even a few other early readers already in, poring over books like *Eton Past and Present, Further Education in Ethiopia in the Eighteenth Century, School Dinners – the Great Debate* and *The History of the Cane.*

"I am looking," whispered Mr Fritz to a librarian who presided over the proceedings, "for a history of Burlap Hall."

"Burlap Hall?" whispered back the librarian. "What's that? Never heard of it."

Mr Fritz felt rather offended. "It's one of the oldest co-educational boarding schools in the entire country," he whispered, as crossly as he could.

The librarian consulted a large book, flicking over pages and running her fingers down endless entries. "Ah, yes," she said finally. "'Burlap Hall – History of.' Afraid it's out with another reader."

"*Out!*" Mr Fritz's yelp startled the other readers who looked up at him crossly. "I'm sorry," he whispered in a tiny voice.

"What?" whispered the librarian.

"I'm sorry!" whispered Mr Fritz back. "May I look at that?" And turning the big book around he saw that *The History of Burlap Hall* was indeed out – and in the possession at that very moment of Woodlouse and Cockroach of Trustus Insurance Company. And looking round he spotted the backs of a couple of horribly familiar heads, gloating over an enormous tome. No doubt they were going over the plans of the school with a magnifying glass, in order to find some good reason not to cough up money for the repairs.

Mr Fritz sighed. His whole trip to London, he felt, had been worthless. He was just turning away feeling most dejected when he heard a faint hissing noise behind him. It was the librarian, whispering again.

"Would you like me to try Schools Cuttings?" she asked. "I'm sure there'd be something about Burlap Hall in old newspaper reports. If it's as famous as you say it is, that is."

It was worth a final shot. Mr Fritz nodded eagerly and was rewarded, half an hour later, by a lad coming round and plonking a small folder of yellowing newspaper cuttings on his desk.

Eagerly Mr Fritz tugged them out. "Burlap Hall gets new science block," he read. "Spanking new image for the oldest co-ed in the North" were the most recent cuttings. Then, some years back: "Burlap Hall on the verge of bankruptcy?" (from the *Times Educational Supplement* 1982). Before that were various boring stories about parents' complaints, pupils who had got to university, sports results, the announcement of Mr Fox as headmaster in 1972, appeal funds for money in 1920, a letter to *The Times* from an old science teacher in 1910 – and that was it. Mr Fritz put his head in his hands. Then he sighed, gathered together the cuttings and slid them back into the folder.

But as he put them back, he felt something. He peered in, and there, at the very bottom, was a scrunched-up cutting that had got squashed by all the others. Gingerly he pulled out the folded strip and carefully smoothed it on the desk.

The cutting was so ancient that the folds were brown and cracked with age. Adjusting his glasses, he saw that the date was January 5th, 1879.

"Head Master of Burlap Hall disappears in Mysterious Circumstances" reported the headline. And underneath, Mr Fritz read the following astonishing story:

The Police Force of Lanchestershire were called to The School of Burlap Hall on Monday to investigate the mysterious Disappearance of the Head Master. Constables were shocked to find Twenty-nine Pupils in a state of great UnderNourishment, and Ragged in Appearance. Several were extremely Sick and some were Near Death. Many were Stained with Blood. It appears that the other School Masters had Run Away, leaving their charges behind.

Mr Horace Squooch, the Head Master, has enjoyed a Difficult Reputation. Several Parents have removed their Sons and Daughters from the School, complaining that Mr Squooch favoured only a few of his Students. To the rest he showed no Mercy and many were treated like Slaves.

Upon Questioning local Inhabitants, Our Earnest Reporter met with little response. The

General Opinion among the Villagers was that Mr Squooch's disappearance was Good Riddance. Mr Jack Tannoy, the local black-smith, said, "The rumour is that the young Gentlemen, in a Frenzy of Rage and Hunger as a result of their Ill Treatment, rose up and beat Mr Squooch to Death."

The Constables have found no body. No Charges will be brought. The School will temporarily be Closed Down.

Those Children who remain whose parents cannot be traced have been taken into the Care of the Parish Council where they will be cared for Kindly until they are old enough to make their Own Way in Life.

Another Mystery that Puzzles the Constabulary is the disappearance of a Sacred Casket from the Church in the grounds of Burlap Hall. If any Person knows of its Whereabouts, will they please inform the Lanchester Constabulary. A reward is Offered.

Mr Fritz shuddered with excitement as he read this. He didn't quite know why, but he just felt a tingle of certainty that this cutting was the key to the whole mystery. He did a little jig by the photo-copying machine as he took copies of his find, and skipped out of the library with a spring in his step.

Back at Burlap Hall at assembly Mr Fox stared

gloomily over a sea of faces. A ray of wintry sunlight filtered through one of the windows and on to Mrs Grain's bun and for some reason the sight made him shudder. At the back of the hall there was a general whispering and giggling until the silence was broken by Signor Ruzzi starting up at the piano. The old piano.

Mr Fox was not in a good mood. The morning's post had brought him two unwelcome letters, and a memo from his staff had really put the lid on matters. As he looked out over the pupils' faces, he wished he'd never set out to be a headmaster in the first place. He should have followed his father's advice and become a banker. By now, no doubt, he would have been the owner of several Rolls Royces, a large town house full of servants, a country mansion and a second home in Barbados.

Instead, what had he got? A school that was falling down around him, a crowd of teachers who were getting less and less satisfied working in surroundings that increasingly resembled a building site, and a collection of the spottiest, dreariest-looking pupils known to man.

As Signor Ruzzi pounded out the old school song on the school piano (a poor substitute for Ruzzi's special home model), Mr Fox pulled his threadbare black gown around him, shivered slightly in the cold, and closed his eyes, trying to imagine himself on the sands of a West Indian island.

But try as he might, nothing could push the memory of those two letters from his mind. The first was from Trustus Insurance.

Dear Sir, it had started. (Didn't they even know his name for heaven's sake?) *Re your insurance claim. Having studied the original plans of the construction of Burlap Hall, checked all records and checked the small print of your policy several times, and as no reason can be found for any of the accidents referred to in your claim, the Trustus Insurance Company deem these accidents an Act of God. Therefore under sub-section 39a, paragraph 2viii, these Acts are not covered by your insurance and as a result we will not be paying you one penny towards their repair.*

Yours sincerely,
Mr Woodlouse and Mr Cockroach

Mr Fox had actually held the letter up to the light, so convinced he was that Woodlouse and Cockroach had added the words: "Ner-ner, ner-ner, ner" in invisible ink at the bottom – but he found nothing.

The second letter had come from the Phantom. No threats were needed this time.

All the Phantom had to do was to write:

SATISFIED? Come tonight. Alone.
Yours,

The Phantom

and Mr Fox realized that now there was no avoiding it. This creature simply had to be met, come what may.

Finally there was the memo from Mr Carstairs on behalf of the staff, expressing what he described as a "crisis of confidence", whatever that might mean, and asking if they could meet him during the first break for a "full and frank discussion" – in other words, just the kind of discussion that Mr Fox always avoided like the plague. "Empty and devious" were how he liked his discussions to be, so that he would have to make no commitments to anyone.

The first break came all too soon and Mr Fox steeled himself for the confrontation. In the Senior Common Room, with its familiar smell of ageing leather, stale smoke and hundreds of cups of old instant coffee, he found himself surrounded by the puzzled, angry faces of his staff. When they were all present, he closed the door on the sounds of the shouting children in the background.

"Before you say anything," he said, as he walked back (he didn't sit down – stay above them and keep the advantage, was his motto), "let me say that I know why you are here." (That was the second tactic. Speak first. Keep in charge of the proceedings.) He waved Mr Carstairs, who had risen with a piece of paper in his hand that looked horribly like a list of complaints, to sit down.

"You are unhappy. I am unhappy. This has been a sad term in the history of Burlap Hall. But all I can ask you is to be patient. I still have not heard from the insurance company." (He had decided it would be better to lie through his teeth; after all, he was going to take the insurance company's letter to a lawyer to see if there was a loophole that could force them to pay up.) "And if by any chance I get a negative response from them, which I doubt, I will certainly appeal. In the mean time I realize how difficult things are for you. Don't think I don't think I don't think I don't." (One too many "don't thinks" in there? He wasn't sure.) "If anything," he added, "I am more unhappy, perplexed and enraged than you." He sat down. He had fired the first salvo.

"I can't sleep easily in bed at night," complained Mrs Grain. "I keep worrying that my classroom is going to collapse. It is affecting my teaching."

"My dear lady," said Mr Fox, gallantly. "I know the feeling. I, too, toss and turn at night. But think of it like the war. Every night we worried that the Germans were coming to bomb us – but we won. We won!"

What, precisely, this had to do with Burlap Hall he didn't quite know, but it seemed to have the desired effect. Colour came to Mrs Grain's cheeks as she nodded her head.

"And the swimming pool!" said Mr Carstairs.

"The swimming pool is one of our biggest tragedies," said Mr Fox. (Secretly he thought: why can't you do without a swimming pool? Ghastly places, full of other people's wee. But he didn't say it.) "It was the pride, like the science block, of Burlap Hall. It was a small princedom in the kingdom of Burlap Hall and you, Mr Carstairs, were the prince. And prince you shall be again. It is just a matter of waiting."

Mr Carstairs looked extremely pleased to be called a prince, and to his relief, Mr Fox saw him putting his sheet of complaints to one side.

"As for our music maestro, Signor Ruzzi, the Beethoven, the Schubert, nay, the Mozart of Burlap Hall – I cannot bear to contemplate the tragedy that has befallen him. I cannot even bear to hear him play on the old piano, it sounds so ... so ... piano, compared to the beautiful instrument he used to possess." (He couldn't bear to hear Signor Ruzzi play on any piano if the truth be told.) "And yet," he added, noticing Signor Ruzzi's moustache bristling dangerously, "our own personal magician of the keys manages to bring life into even the dead and battered old piano of yesteryear. Genius ... maestro ... I salute you!" He started clapping his hands and immediately everyone in the room followed. Signor Ruzzi's angry frown burst into a beam of delight.

"As for the rest of you, indeed all of us, the anxiety and worry linger like storm-clouds over our lives. Times are dark for Burlap Hall, times are frightening and menacing. The threat of disaster follows us like the will-o-the-wisp of destiny," (It sounded good – heaven knows what it meant.) "and it is only with the courage, the determination, the bravery and the sheer," – here he got to his feet – "*guts* that everyone at Burlap Hall is famous for, that we will win through!" Throwing up a fist in a punching motion at the ceiling, he started singing the school song, spontaneously and unaccompanied:

"Oh Burlap Hall, oh Burlap Hall,
Our pupils are so strong and tall!
Our hungry minds, feast on our books,
Our splendid brains, match noble looks!
Oh Burlap Hall, oh Burlap Hall,
Our pupils are so strong and tall!"

"Again!" And signalling for all the teachers to rise he got them to join him in a second verse. To his amazement, they did just that and, at the end, they all gave a "Hip! Hip! Hurrah!"; Miss Shepherd murmured, "I have a dream..."; Mrs Grain roared, "We will fight them on the beaches..."; Mr Roy started shrieking, "Down with animal experiments! Up Burlap Hall!"; Signor Ruzzi, completely carried away, shouted, "Viva Garibaldi!" and Mr Carstairs jumped on to a table shouting, "Uhuru! We will win through!"

Mr Fox, while shaking everyone's hand as they filtered back to their lessons, gave himself a mental pat on the back. That, he said to himself, was what they call a close shave. He couldn't do that again, either. But wasn't it amazing, he thought to himself, what the powers of oratory could do? As he walked down the corridor to his office he found himself humming the Burlap Hall school song until he pulled himself together. He might fool the teachers, but he really couldn't fool himself. They were in a terrible mess. But just as his spirits were beginning to sink, he was heartened to see Mr Fritz, hurrying along the corridor with a sheaf of papers under his arm.

"My dear chap," he said, hastening to greet him. "How good to see you! Come into the office!"

And with his finger to his lips he ushered the science teacher to a chair and sat down behind his desk. Speaking softly, he said, "Mr Fritz! Pessimissimus! I haven't yet told the rest of the staff but between you and me – the Trustus Insurance Company have turned us down!"

Mr Fritz's face fell. "Oh, Headmaster!" he said. "That's too bad! I saw Woodlouse and Cockroach themselves looking at *The History of Burlap Hall* in the library, so clearly they've been doing their research. I hope you'll appeal."

"I will – but what hope is there against an insurance company?"

Mr Fritz was silent. "And the – er – our friend?"

Mr Fox tossed the latest piece of parchment over to Mr Fritz. "I'll have to meet him tonight."

Mr Fritz looked at the Phantom's note and nodded. "I wonder..." he murmured to himself.

Then he drew out a copy of the cutting he'd found at the British Library and showed it to Mr Fox. Mr Fox read it, frowned, and pushed it back.

"So? This hardly makes things any clearer, does it?"

"I was wondering," said Mr Fritz, "whether the Phantom and Mr Horace Squooch couldn't be one and the same person."

Mr Fox scratched his head. "My dear chap, look at the date of the cutting! Mr Horace Squooch would be something like, er, a

hundred and fifty years old! Anyway, he probably died in 1879!"

"I was thinking, er, of his ghost," said Mr
Fritz.

"His ghost! And you, a science teacher! Why
only the other day you were pooh-poohing the
idea! You implied there were no such things as
ghosts!"

"I suppose not," said Mr Fritz uncertainly,
putting the cutting back into his pocket. He
sighed. He got up. "Well, I wish you all the luck
in the world with your meeting tonight. I'm so
sorry the Phantom has insisted that no one goes
with you. Otherwise I would have been the first
to offer..." He could hardly keep the relief out
of his voice as he leant forward and shook Mr
Fox's hand. He did it in such a way that
Mr Fox suddenly felt frightened. He hoped Mr
Fritz wasn't saying goodbye to him for ever.

"I – er – will come and see you straight after
the meeting," said Mr Fox hopefully. "Though
it might be rather late, of course."

"By all means," said Mr Fritz, shaking his
head as he left the study.

Mr Fritz had a much more positive response to
his findings from Tom and Miles when he
asked them up to his room later that day.

"You're right!" whistled Tom when he'd
read the cutting. "Mr Horace Squooch! He's
the Phantom! Ugh, he must be horrible!"

108

"What do you think he wants from Mr Fox, I wonder?" asked Miles, scratching his head.

"I expect he'll find out tonight, after ... oh dear," added Mr Fritz. "I'm being indiscreet."

"So Mr Fox is going to meet the Phantom tonight, is he?" said Tom. "Are you going with him?"

"No, no," said Mr Fritz hastily. "I'm far too busy. I mean tired. I mean, old. Er ... well, to tell you the truth I don't really fancy the idea. And anyway," he added, remembering, "he said Mr Fox had to come alone."

Tom looked at Miles and Miles looked at Tom and they both nodded at each other.

"He may think he's alone," said Tom, "but he won't be."

Mr Fritz looked shocked. "I don't think that's wise, boys..." he said.

"But how are you going to be sure Mr Fox tells you the truth unless you've got independent witnesses to this meeting?" said Miles. "You can't trust Mr Fox an inch."

"Or a millimetre," said Tom.

"Or a squillimetre," said Miles, not be outdone.

"I have to say," said Mr Fritz solemnly, "that I think it would be a great mistake for you to go."

"We'll put it to the vote," said Tom. "All those in favour raise their hands." He and Miles put up with their hands.

"All those against?" Mr Fritz put his hand up very half-heartedly. "Oh, all right," he said, putting it down. "But this Squooch sounds a dangerous character. So promise me – take care."

CHAPTER SEVEN

That night, as Mr Fox saw the hands on his clock approach midnight, his heart sank into his boots. It was an impossible situation – one minute he felt terrified of meeting the Phantom and the next he felt a complete fool because, after all, he didn't believe in the supernatural, so how could he be afraid? Each emotion followed the next in an endless cycle – terror followed by a slap of good sense followed by terror and so on. Still, there was no getting out of it now. He'd have to face the music.

He slipped softly out of his room and down the stairs to the front door. He didn't hear the faint rustle of Tom and Miles' slippered footsteps as they tiptoed after him through the darkness.

Mr Fox unlocked the front door; as it swung open it creaked on its hinges. Out into the crisp night air he went – and after him, through the crack in the dark, slipped Tom and Miles, vanishing swiftly in some bushes near by.

Nothing moved. The moon was a silvery circle in the sky, painting the branches of the leafless trees with a thin metallic light. Mr Fox peered into the darkness. He could see nothing. All he was aware of, suddenly, was a terrible smell. A smell of drains.

Tom and Miles smelt it too and Tom nudged Miles angrily.

"Not me!" whispered Miles. "It's that smell, don't you remember? It's him. The Phantom."

And suddenly, there he was. He seemed to have appeared out of nowhere, as if a silent handclap had simply introduced him – or it – on to the path in front of Mr Fox.

Mr Fox practically leapt out of his skin. He was speechless.

Then, since the Phantom said nothing, Mr Fox put out his hand nervously. "Ah, the Phantom, I presume?" he said. "We had an appointment to meet. I am Mr Fox, headmaster of Burlap Hall."

The Phantom, who was in the middle of thrusting out a bony cloak-covered arm towards Mr Fox's hand, suddenly jerked it back at the words.

"Headmaster of Burlap Hall! I beg to differ, sir!" he said. And his voice was as old, oily and smelly as black slime. "*I* am the headmaster of Burlap Hall!"

But Mr Fox was engaged in his own reactions.

"Excuse me!" he said, drawing himself up. "But *I* am the headmaster of Burlap Hall!"

"If you continue to think of yourself that way," said the Phantom, in a threatening voice, "there will be no more Burlap Hall for you to be headmaster of! *I* am the headmaster.

I am the *true* headmaster. I am Horace Squooch and I was deprived of my post by wicked, illegal crimes. Therefore I am still headmaster of Burlap Hall."

("So Mr Fritz was right!" said Tom. "It's Horace Squooch himself!" Miles shook his head in wonderment. "Horace Squooch's ghost!" he said.)

"Horace Squooch!" breathed Mr Fox. "You're that old devil who got lynched to death by his pupils! But you can't be! It's too long ago!" Then, as the truth of the ghostly nature of his visitor slowly dawned on him, he gulped.

The Phantom stood in front of him, a sheet of blackness. He said nothing. He just stared at Mr Fox through two tiny slits in his hooded cloak.

"What do you want?" breathed Mr Fox.

"I want my rights," said the Phantom.

"What rights?" asked Mr Fox.

"My rights as headmaster. I propose to continue to run Burlap Hall – but through you. You will appear to be the headmaster. But in fact I am the headmaster, and you will do nothing, impose no new rules or make any alterations to the school curriculum without consulting me."

Mr Fox relaxed visibly. "But that's fine!" he said, sighing with relief. "I've got no plans for changing the curriculum. So that's

113

it, eh? No changes without consulting you? Excellent. Now perhaps you will leave us alone." He stretched out his hand for a farewell shake.

"No changes to the school curriculum *once you have changed it to the way I would like it to be*!" hissed the Phantom.

Mr Fox paused. He rubbed his hands together to get some circulation going. It was dreadfully cold standing out there in the middle of the night.

"Like what?" he asked.

"I have prepared a list," said the Phantom, drawing a piece of paper from the folds of his black cloak. "If, by the end of this week, all my new proposals have been instigated, then all well and good. If not..."

"There is hardly any more of the school for you to pull down, old chap!" said Mr Fox trying to be jovial as he took the yellowed parchment.

But the Phantom just looked at him coldly. "Oh yes there is," he said, in a menacing voice. "Now study that list carefully. That is just the beginning. I will be in touch with you concerning further developments. I repeat. Initiate all these practices and no more will happen to the school. Fail to initiate them and you do so at your peril!" With a swirl of his black cloak, he turned on his heel and vanished.

In the darkness Mr Fox was left studying the

list. Quietly he read it out to himself – but not so quietly that Tom and Miles couldn't hear.

"Children will have to scrub the floors and do the washing up. Only one meal a day. Turn heating off completely except in staff rooms and those of my favoured pupil – Susan, the red-headed American girl – strict punishments, no communication with parents ... hmm," said Mr Fox as he stuffed the list into his jacket pocket. "Might have a bit of trouble getting that through. Still, some of his ideas aren't at all bad. Save on heating *and* food." Then, slapping his hands to his sides to warm himself, he slipped back into the school and locked the door behind him.

Tom and Miles stared at each other, shocked. "He can't mean to carry out those orders for the Phantom?" said Tom. "That sort of thing isn't allowed these days, surely!"

Miles shook his head. "I wouldn't put anything past Mr Fox," he said gloomily as he approached the front door. Then he stopped. "Hang on!" he said. "We're locked out!"

Tom thought for a moment. Then, "Come on," he said. "Mr Fritz will still be up! He'll let us in!"

They rushed round the side of the building and sure enough, the light was still on in Mr Fritz's room. After they'd thrown a few stones up at the window, it was opened and Mr Fritz peered down.

"Oh, it's you!" he said. "I can't come down. I'm waiting for Mr Fox!"

"But we're dying of cold!" whispered Tom.

With a lot of cross muttering, Mr Fritz left the window and returned with a sheet which he lowered down. "You'll have to scramble up on that, I'm afraid," he said.

"No problem," said Miles, grabbing it and starting to winch himself up. "Now I know what that sports practice of Carstairs was all about."

Tom followed and just as they landed in a tumbled heap on Mr Fritz's floor there was a knock at the door.

"Quick! Hide in the cupboard!" said Mr Fritz. And as he shut the cupboard on the two boys, in walked Mr Fox.

"Window open in this weather?" said Mr Fox suspiciously, shivering at the howling draught that was blowing through the room. "You weren't spying on us were you?"

"Certainly not, Headmaster," said Mr Fritz rather huffily as he shut it. "I keep the window open for health reasons. And anyway, surely your meeting was on the other side of the building."

"True," said Mr Fox. But he didn't look convinced.

"So – I've put the kettle on for a cuppa," said Mr Fritz bustling round with some teabags, "and look forward to hearing..."

"Have you got nothing stronger, man?" asked Mr Fox, looking nervous and cold.

"Coffee?" suggested Mr Fritz cheerfully.

"No – spirits. Alcohol. A drink for heaven's sake!"

Mr Fritz scratched his head. "Alcohol, alcohol. There's the alcohol we use for scientific experiments but I don't think you'd like that..."

"You want to pickle me?" said Mr Fox, angrily. "No thanks! It would kill me!"

"Wait a minute! There's some ginger wine my aunt gave me for Christmas..." Mr Fritz rummaged in a cupboard and produced the bottle.

"Capital!" said Mr Fox seizing it and pouring himself a tumblerful. He knocked it back. "Excellent. Well, I've got good news. There's nothing to worry about at all. This Phantom – he seemed a pleasant enough chap. Said he used to be Horace Squooch – you were right on the button on that one if I may say (yes, another glass would be excellent) and that all he wanted were a few – er – a few um, alterations, and then he'd call off his troops. I mean, you know, stop doing those things he's been doing."

Mr Fritz looked very suspicious. "What alterations?" he asked.

"Oh, nothing, nothing," said Mr Fox, looking rather uncomfortable. "Small things.

117

You'll see in the next few days. Soon we'll have everything sorted out." And then, taking a final swig of the last drops of ginger wine, he beat a hasty retreat to bed.

The minute he'd shut the door the two boys tumbled out of the cupboard.

"Liar!" hissed Tom, pointing an accusing finger.

"Scumbag!" growled Miles as he disentangled one of Mr Fritz's old walking sticks that had got caught up with his dressing-gown cord.

"Boys, boys, sssh, sssh!" said Mr Fritz, rather shocked. "Calm down! Have a cup of tea. Oh dear," he said, as he removed the empty ginger wine bottle from the table. "And I was rather looking forward to enjoying that in the coming months. Oh well." Sadly he dropped it into the wastepaper basket.

"He's going to change the school back into how it was in the old days," said Miles. "Punishments, all the pupils doing the housework, no lessons, slave labour!"

"No heating! One meal a day!" said Tom. "Just like those awful Yorkshire schools Mrs Grain was telling us about!"

Mr Fritz smiled amusedly as he handed them mugs of tea. "Oh, surely not," he said. "Mr Fox may be a bit of a..." He thought better of saying what the headmaster might be a bit of and continued, "But deep down he is good-hearted and caring."

118

The howling silence that emanated from Tom and Miles took the kindly smile off his face. "And anyway, why do you say he's a liar? What did you hear?"

Tom and Miles told the science teacher, over steaming mugs of tea, all they knew, and as they talked Mr Fritz's face become serious. "Oh dear," he kept saying. "Oh dear. Oh dear. Yes, I see. Oh dear."

Finally he shook his head. "All we can do now is wait to see what Mr Fox's next move is. But I'm glad you went along. He doesn't know that we're one jump ahead of him."

Outside the assembly hall the next morning Susan seemed to be in a trance. She stood by the door waiting for the bell with her eyes fixed on the ceiling, muttering to herself. When Tom and Miles approached, she seemed unaware of their presence.

"*Cogito, ergo sum*," she said. "The square on the hypotenuse equals the sum of the squares of the other two sides. Archimedes' principle – when a body is weighed in air and then in any fluid, the apparent loss in weight is equal to the weight of fluid displaced. Mozart was born in 1756."

"Susan?" said Miles. "Are you all right?"

"The basis of papal infallibility is that every question of morals and faith is not dealt with in the Bible so it is necessary that there should

119

be a sure court of appeal in case of doubt," replied Susan. "The doctrine was claimed in 1870."

"Susan!" said Tom.

"Did you know," said Susan, looking at him vaguely, "that James Joyce, born 1882, was an Irish author who created a new form of the novel? In *Portrait of the Artist as a Young Man*, which he wrote in 1916, he covers the childhood and adolescence of a writer. In *Ulysses*, published in 1922..."

Luckily the bell rang and her trance seemed to be broken. "Why are you staring at me, you guys?" she suddenly snapped. "Never seen a girl before?"

"You were talking to yourself!" whispered Miles.

"I wasn't!"

"You were!" whispered Miles.

"Rubbish!" Susan flushed.

"Don't get hysterical," said Miles.

"Hersterical!" said Susan, back briefly to her normal self.

Mr Fox had wrestled long and hard during the past night over how on earth to put the Phantom's ideas into practice. At the end of assembly he coughed and announced that he had a big surprise for the school, which would involve some radical changes.

"About time too," whispered Asquith Minor.

"Now, now!" said Mr Fox reprovingly, clapping his hands for silence. "These changes are about the environment."

Tom and Miles looked at each other in astonishment. What had the environment to do with the Phantom's ideas?

"It has occurred to me that it would be an interesting test to see how we could cut down on energy," proceeded Mr Fox. "And it is for this reason, to save the planet from extinction, that I propose we should make do for the rest of the term without heat."

"Without heat!" Mrs Grain exploded from the back of the assembly stage. "We'll freeze to death!"

"We will not freeze to death!" said Mr Fox sharply. "We will be cold, true. But we will also be preserving the ozone layer. Given the choice of the extinction of the world and being just a teeny weeny bit cold, I know what your answer will be: save the world!"

A cheer went up from the children in the front, a cheer which spread through the hall. It was a good feeling, saving the environment, no doubt about that.

"And we must preserve paper, as well, because paper uses up valuable trees," said Mr Fox. "So I propose that in future we write on both sides of our paper during classes – and that for this term at least you forfeit writing home."

There was a howl of disappointment from Sheila, who looked forward to letters from her mum and dad.

"You'll see your parents in the holidays. But if you would prefer to write to them than save the rainforests, that's fine by me," said Mr Fox, pursing his lips and looking up to the ceiling.

"Shame!" called a boy from the front. And eventually Sheila had to agree to stop writing to her parents. Her eyes, however, were misty at the thought.

"I am worried, too, about the Third World, where children are starving. Children get only one meal a week, if that, in some parts of the world – and here we are, having three meals a day – or four if you count tea. I propose that we cut our meals down to one a day and that we send the money we have saved to the starving in India."

"We'll be so hungry!" said Tom who, as a growing boy, never really thought that four meals were enough during the day. About ten would suit him nicely in fact.

"It's up to you. If you want to gorge yourselves while children starve and die – fine!" Mr Fox looked round at the whole school with folded arms, whistling a little tune.

"Come on, Tom, we can't let children starve," said Simon from the front, turning round. Tom shrugged. It sounded a dreadful idea to him. Particularly as he knew that

122

Mr Fox's motives had absolutely nothing to do with saving starving children.

"Now, since you will have a little less energy, as your bodies will be coping with the cold and lack of food, we will cut down drastically on lessons," said Mr Fox. He had left this master-stroke till last, knowing that it would get a good reception.

"Hurrah!" The sound of children cheering was so loud it could have been heard in Lanchester. It was so loud that it drowned the feeble protests from the teachers behind him, who were outraged at the idea that their lessons should be cut. When Mr Fox flounced off the podium he brushed aside their criticisms.

"My dear Carstairs, this is an ecological experiment," he said. "Let's see how it works out before we start to criticize, shall we? As for you, Mr Roy, I'm ashamed of you. You should be the first to support me in such a revolutionary experiment, since it touches precisely on the very subject you teach, geography! Goodness me, Signor Ruzzi, not you as well! How is great art born if not through suffering? And Mrs Grain and Miss Shepherd, I suggest you both think before you speak!" And with that, he swept off into his study where he immediately turned his electric fire on to high, put his feet on his desk, and started reading the papers.

* * *

The next fortnight was the worst in the living memory of Burlap Hall – just as bad as it had been in the days when it was run by Horace Squooch himself. Children stayed in bed all day to keep warm – until, according to the wishes of the Phantom, Mr Fox ordered them up and removed their blankets "to send to the poor people in Africa" (in other words to be stored in the garage). Everyone started losing weight and getting ill – and by the end of the first week most of the kids were longing for the old routine, lessons and all.

On the instructions of the Phantom, Mr Fox had set the smaller children the task of clearing up the rubble that was once the science block – a backbreaking job out in the cold which involved small children heaping carts high with bricks and dragging them to a large lorry where they would have to be stacked before being taken away. The meals – or rather meal – got smaller and smaller by the day until, by the end of the second week, most of the children were living on one slice of toast a day and one cup of Heinz tomato soup.

At first, Mr Fox tried to resist the Phantom's more severe demands. OK, OK, he felt, the Phantom had some jolly good ideas. But the blanket nonsense was going a bit far. Why shouldn't the children have some warmth at night?

But one look from the Phantom and Mr Fox

was powerless. It was partly the sheer force of the Phantom's personality, but mainly the fear of the whole school being pulled down around his ears, that kept Mr Fox a slave to the creature's wishes.

As for the teachers, he could handle most of the protests for the time being. It was quite easy to make all the teachers who complained feel guilty. He kept promising them that the experiment would last only a short time and that it was worth going along with it for the sake of ecology and the environment.

The only person he knew he could not handle was Mr Fritz. Mr Fritz constantly talked about things like Schools' Inspectors as if he intended to get them in. So when Mr Fox got another note from the Phantom telling him to get rid of the science teacher he was, in one way, relieved, and in another way, appalled.

And when Mr Fritz finally went to complain for the fifth time, he was met by a headmaster who welcomed him into his study with an unpleasant, frightened glint in his eye.

"Any complaints, Fritz?" he said sharply. My goodness, thought Mr Fritz, he's almost turning into Horace Squooch himself. "Do you object to my saving the world? If so, just say so!"

"Headmaster," said Mr Fritz, sitting down, "this cannot go on."

"*This* cannot go on, or *you* cannot go on?"

asked Mr Fox tartly, producing from a desk drawer a steaming chicken pie which he had purchased half an hour earlier from the town. He bit into it.

"Both," said Mr Fritz.

Mr Fox decided he was absolutely no good at this kind of sacking thing. Although he may have appeared tough and ruthless, inside he was like jelly. But like all weak men, while he could never have sacked Mr Fritz off his own bat – nor would he have wanted to, come to that – he simply couldn't refuse the Phantom's orders. And it was such an unpleasant task he had to perform, he wanted to get it over with as soon as possible.

"Well, I have the perfect answer to your problem!" he snapped, through mouthfuls of chicken. "Leave! You're free to go. If you don't like it here, just buzz off!" Inside, he felt dreadfully ashamed of his behaviour.

"Headmaster!" said Mr Fritz, getting up. "Surely you don't mean..."

"I do!" said Mr Fox. "I have your final cheque here in a drawer, in fact." He wrenched out a pile of papers and handed them to Mr Fritz. "Thank you for all your invaluable work, etc.," he said, "and goodbye."

Mr Fritz felt the room spin. He took the papers in disbelief.

"But you can't mean..." He looked down at the papers and saw, sticking out from under his

National Insurance card, a slip of yellow parchment. He pulled it out. On it was written in the Phantom's spidery hand: *Start getting rid of the teachers! Too much expense! First – the science master!*

"You mean – the Phantom has ordered you to fire me!" he said. "Mr Fox, I never thought that you, of all people, would..."

"Thank you very much," said Mr Fox, wiping the crumbs of pie from his lips. "No discussion please. Thank you and goodbye."

Mr Fritz turned, shocked, to the door. "You won't hear the last of this, you know," he said threateningly. "I'll be back!"

"I don't think you will," replied Mr Fox, with a fearful look on his face. "The Phantom has many powers and if I were you I wouldn't chance my arm against him."

Mr Fritz went white. As he made his way to his room his knees were like jelly. He passed groups of children huddling together in the cold, stretching out their hands for a biscuit Mr Fritz might be able to give them. But Mr Fritz just shut his eyes. He couldn't face thinking about the situation any more. He went into his room, got out his suitcase and started to pack. Within an hour he had left, without saying goodbye to anybody. He had never felt so betrayed in his life and he couldn't face any of the other teachers witnessing his humiliation and anger.

Meanwhile, in his study, Mr Fox put his head in his hands and, with a groan, muttered, "Oh, pessimissimus!"

Firing Mr Fritz had been the worst moment of Mr Fox's life. He had cut off his only lifeline to sanity. In the days following, he was racked with guilt, often wishing that Mr Fritz had left a forwarding address so that he could contact him and ask him to come back. They'd face the Phantom together. But then, another part of of him argued, what else could he have done? If he'd kept Fritz on, the Phantom would have pulled the entire school down. In those circumstances there would be no job for Mr Fritz or any of the other teachers anyway.

As for Tom and Miles, they were appalled when they learned that Mr Fritz had left. First they thought he'd simply left because he was ill, or that he'd gone off on some personal trip. They thought he'd be back. But then the rumours started to fly and after a few days they learned the truth.

"But how could he have abandoned us like that?" said Tom. "Without even saying goodbye!"

"Do you think he's really gone?" said Miles worriedly. "I mean, you don't think the Phantom might have – well, you, know, got rid of him, um, properly."

"You mean... Oh, Miles, we've got to do something!"

They were huddled, along with several other children, outside Susan's door. Susan was allowed to have heating and meals, and at least the outside of her door was warm. Her door was locked and no one was allowed in to see her. From within could be heard nothing but her reciting facts from the encyclopaedia.

"Yes, this isn't some temporary experiment," said Miles, through chattering teeth. "It's going to go on and on, and it's going to get worse. Let's run away and tell our parents. If we could only find a phone box we could ask them to come and see for themselves what's happening."

Tom nodded. "After tea," he said.

"What tea?" asked Miles gloomily. "There is none, remember?"

There was no problem getting away from the school even though it was dark. They ran in their thin clothes, now torn and ragged, down to the village. A few people looked at them in dismay, not recognizing them as pupils of Burlap Hall. The phone box had been vandalized so it meant going on to the next village, a long walk in the cold. But eventually they managed to contact Tom's mother.

"Tom, I just can't believe what you're saying," said Mrs Buxton, when Tom explained the situation. "Burlap Hall is a school with an excellent reputation. You've never been unhappy there before!"

"I'm not just unhappy, Mum," said Tom, almost crying with the cold. "I'm freezing and I'm hungry and we're not learning anything. Please come and take me away!"

"I'll certainly come and try to sort things out," promised Mrs Buxton. "Because even though I can't believe what you're saying I can hear you're distressed. So I'll see you tomorrow afternoon."

Miles' parents were out and the two boys trundled sadly back to Burlap Hall – now in pitch darkness since the electricity had been turned off.

But little did they know what had happened at the school in their absence.

When Mrs Buxton had rung the headmaster, five minutes after Tom's phone call, to find out the times of trains, Mr Fox had, initially, been extremely relieved. Her call seemed to solve everything. If a parent was visiting, then surely even the Phantom would agree that everything had to be back to normal? But no sooner had he rushed down to the electricity switch and turned it on, and no sooner were the lights blazing in the classrooms and hot water gurgling into the pipes (accompanied by screams of delight from the frozen pupils), than there was a loud knocking at the door.

With a pounding heart, Mr Fox went down the corridor to open it. He had an awful feeling he knew exactly who it was. And he was right. There, his eyes flashing in the darkness, was the Phantom, fizzing with fury.

"What is the meaning of this!?" he exploded as he forced his way in. "Heat! Light! I told you what would happen if you went against me!"

"But – but," said Mr Fox, backing away. "You see, the parents of one of the boys are complaining. And coming to visit. So we have to get things back to normal by tomorrow. OK?"

"OK? OK?" The Phantom seemed to grow in stature as he towered over Mr Fox. "It is not 'OK' as you say! Now go and snuff out all those candles you must have lit. At once! And dampen down the fires. A waste of wax and wood! And get a message to this parent and tell him his son has died! That's the way to deal with them. Short and sharp!"

"Died!" gasped Mr Fox. "But you can't..."

The Phantom hissed with anger. "Can't? Can't? What's wrong with the odd death? The numbers of boys who died during my time at Burlap Hall – well, there are too many to remember all their names. You are far too sensitive, Mr Fox, that's your problem. You cannot accept that death is simply another form of discipline!"

131

"It's his mother," said Mr Fox, shutting his eyes with a mixture of horror and misery, as he heard the Phantom's last remarks.

"I don't care who it is! I don't care how you do it!" snapped the Phantom. "But give this parent the message and make sure no parent visits tomorrow! Or ever! Or," he added warningly, gripping Mr Fox's arm with a steely grasp, "there won't be a school to visit. And then you'll have a lot more than one parent to explain to! Heh heh! Now off you go! Deal with it!"

Mr Fox wrung his hands. The situation was absolutely terrible! He just didn't know what to do! He rang Mrs Buxton back and explained that he'd only just found out that Tom had flu and had been hallucinating ... and he didn't know how many other preposterous lies he told to put her off. But with the threat of his beloved school going for ever, he became more fluent by the minute. Finally she seemed satisfied with his explanations and agreed not to come up. She just wanted Tom to call her.

By the time Tom and Miles returned, Mr Fox had completely caved in. He felt utterly powerless. If only tomorrow morning he could wake up and find all this a bad dream! In the mean time he was prepared to do anything the Phantom wanted. He was, simply, terrorized.

So when the two boys returned, shivering

quietly up the stairs to their room, they were met with the angry tones of Mr Fox on the top landing.

"Tom! Miles! What is the meaning of this!"

Worse, behind him stood the Phantom, glowering, a black sheet of darkness that emanated terror and hate.

"Your mother rang me to find out the times of trains and it was only with great difficulty that I managed to put her off," said Mr Fox, approaching dangerously. He hardly knew what he was saying. He just knew he had to appear ruthless in front of the Phantom or the consequences would be disastrous. "As a result of this action, you certainly won't go home for the holidays. You may never go home again, in fact!"

Tom felt all the stuffing knocked out of him in a single blow. Never go home again? Then who could help him? Tom looked round for Miles, who had gone green.

"Now, your punishment," gabbled Mr Fox wildly, pointing at the Phantom. "This gentleman has kindly agreed to select a punishment for you, although he is extremely busy."

The black shape stared at them through his slits. Then the Phantom spoke. "You will have no supper, you will stay out in the cold all night, and when you return in the morning you will be beaten within an inch of your lives. I think that that is a fair and rather lenient punishment in the circumstances, don't you, Mr Fox?"

A final grain of humanity forced Mr Fox to intervene.

"Two inches of their lives?" he begged, rather weakly.

"Pah! Half an inch for daring to contradict me, Mr Fox!" replied the Phantom. His eyes glittered with madness while Tom and Miles clung to each other, quivering with fear and cold. Mr Fox stood by dumbly, unable to say anything.

"Now out!" snapped the Phantom. "Out! You must learn the meaning of discipline!"

Tom and Miles tumbled down the stairs and back through the front door. Behind them they heard the lock turning and footsteps going back up the stairs inside.

"What can we do?" said Tom, in despair.

Miles shook his head. "Do you think that Susan...?"

They looked up towards her window. It glowed warmly above them in the night and they could just make out the silhouette of her frizzy head, bowed over a book. Tom picked up some gravel to throw at the window but Miles pulled his arm. "No – look!" he said. And glancing up they saw the black shape of the Phantom entering her room and picking up a huge book.

"It's no good," said Miles, looking round. "There's no shelter or anything. I can't see how we're going to survive the night."

"All we can do is crawl into some bushes, huddle up close, sleep for perhaps a few hours and then try to get away in the morning," said Tom, heading for a large rhododendron bush. "Come on in here. It's not exactly cosy but it's sheltered."

They sat down together and pulled some branches and leaves round them. Then Miles said, "I'm sure we shouldn't sleep. Not in this cold. I mean, I think you can die if you sleep in the cold. That's what my dad says, anyway."

"Oh, Miles, what are we going to do?" wailed Tom, suddenly clinging to his friend.

"I don't know!" sobbed Miles, clutching him back. "There just seems no way out!"

CHAPTER EIGHT

As Tom and Miles huddled together, they didn't hear the crunch of footsteps on the path. But when the noise stopped, they looked up as the branches above them were parted and a black shape emerged from above.

"Oh, don't hurt us!" pleaded Tom and Miles.

The black shape pushed further into the bush and suddenly in the moonlight a figure became clear. The moon cast light on a friendly ginger beard and a prickly brown suit and some sharp eyes twinkling through half-moon glasses... It was Mr Fritz.

"Great heavens!" he said, pulling the boys out of the bushes. "What are you doing here at this time of night!"

The relief of seeing Mr Fritz was almost too much for Tom and Miles. For a few moments they were unable to speak. Then, "Oh, please take us away from here, Mr Fritz!" said Miles. "Mr Fox has gone completely mad and is in the power of the Phantom. We're being punished for trying to run away!"

"Punished! Why! Look at the state of you! When did you last eat?" Mr Fritz's eyes were full of indignant outrage as he eyed them up and down. He stretched out a hand to help them up.

"The day before yesterday, sir," said Tom. "Or was it the day before that? I can't remember!" But those were the last words he spoke because at that moment he fainted.

Tom woke to find himself in the back of Mr Fritz's old Morris van with both his friend and teacher looking anxiously down at him.

Once he saw Tom had recovered, Mr Fritz got into the driving seat. He revved the engine. "First of all, some food and drink," he said. "But where on earth will be open? It's eleven o'clock and round here they roll up the streets at ten."

"I think there's a Chinese in Lanchester," said Miles nervously. He'd been there once with his dad late at night when returning to school after a half-term.

"Excellent!" said Mr Fritz, roaring out of the drive.

In the empty restaurant and over a hot meal – in fact the first proper meal they'd had in days – they explained to Mr Fritz what had happened since he'd left. Mr Fritz could hardly believe it. And at the end he pushed away his food half-eaten and put his head in his hands.

"I had no idea that things would get this bad so fast," he said. "I feel so ashamed of myself."

Tom took Mr Fritz's plate and spooned half the sweet and sour pork, crispy noodles and Peking duck on to his plate and half on to

Miles'. "It's not your fault, sir," he said. "It's Mr Fox's."

"Or Horace Squooch's," said Miles, with his mouth full as he stretched for more soy sauce. He nodded at the waiter when he asked if they wanted more rice.

"It was a matter of principle that I couldn't stay after Mr Fox had fired me, of course," said Mr Fritz, pulling himself together. "And also because of a fit of temper, I have to admit. I should have just hung on there and waited for the police to move me out. Then none of this would have happened. But anyway, after a few days I realized that I couldn't live with myself, leaving a dangerous situation like that behind. So I returned tonight to see how things were and to have a word with Mr Fox. But as I walked up the drive, I heard you talking in the bushes and decided to investigate."

"And thank goodness you did, sir," said Tom, heaping mounds from the new bowl of rice on to his plate. "Or we might have been dead by now."

Miles shuddered. "But what are we going to do?" he asked, looking through the menu at the puddings. ("Crispy deep-fried apple covered in honey and sesame seeds," he said to the waiter. Tom nodded in agreement. He couldn't speak, his mouth was too full.) "I mean it's all very well for us, but everyone else at the school is in much the same position.

Not out in the cold, but desperately hungry."

"Except for Susan," said Tom, scraping the last bit of sauce from the plate. "She's allowed everything. She's the Phantom's favourite and completely in his power."

Mr Fritz frowned in thought. "I wonder if we should go back after the meal and try to sort it out? Or stay in a bed and breakfast and go tomorrow morning?"

"Tomorrow morning the Phantom won't be around," said Miles. "He was there tonight but I've never seen him in the day."

"And Mr Fox will have a hangover which will make him easier to deal with," said Mr Fritz.

"And now everyone will be asleep," said Tom. "Tomorrow you can see the state they're in."

"Aren't the other teachers doing anything?" said Mr Fritz as he signalled for the bill.

"I think they're catching on," said Miles. "But Mr Fox still seems to be pulling the old environmental wool over their eyes."

"He's playing on everyone's guilt," said Tom. "And to be honest, none of the teachers knew what was happening to us tonight. I don't think they'd have gone along with it."

"I should hope not!" said Mr Fritz. "Right, we'll find a bed and breakfast, and tomorrow we'll face the music!"

* * *

Back at Burlap Hall Mr Fox was having a sleepless night. He was terribly worried that Tom and Miles might not survive the night. When he'd been sure the Phantom had gone back to wherever he went to, he'd crept out and searched the grounds, planning to bring Tom and Miles back into the school for the night, give them a good bowl of soup, keep them hidden in his study, pop them outside in the morning and hope to be able to persuade the Phantom out of the beating in the morning. But search as he might, he could find no trace of them. Either they'd run away again or they'd already died and were lying, frozen and stiff, under a bush. Mr Fox shuddered in his bed. He could see the headlines now:

HEADMASTER SENTENCED TO LIFE IMPRISONMENT FOR MANSLAUGHTER OF TWO PUPILS.

Shamed headmaster Mr Fox, bowed his head as he received his sentence and said, in court, "I deserve everything. I have lost my career and my self-respect. I am a ruined man." The sobbing parents of the two boys said, "Justice has at last been done." Never in its infamous history since the Victorian headmaster, Horace Squooch, died in mysterious circumstances, has there been a headmaster quite as evil as Mr Eric Fox. Born of humble parents...

As he imagined this report, Mr Fox's heart beat faster with panic and shame. He even found tears springing to his eyes – whether for the fate of the boys or himself he did not know. In a final frenzy of tormented conscience, he jumped out of bed and pulled on his clothes for one last search of the grounds.

But though he looked for over an hour – in the bushes, by the pond, past the tennis courts, through the wood, even daring to call their names softly in the darkness – there was still no sign of the boys.

Not even bodies.

Cursing himself and his own weakness, Mr Fox finally stumbled back to the school and got into bed, haunted by thoughts of the consequences of his actions and bitter regret at having got himself in so deep with the Phantom. If only he hadn't sacked Mr Fritz! *He*'d know what to do! Mr Fox knew he'd been far too hasty. Or if only he could persuade the Phantom to bring his ideas up-to-date! But there was no hope of that. Mr Fox even toyed with the idea of waking the staff and confessing everything. But who would believe him? And anyway, he'd lose such face, after all that ecological talk. It was all too, too frightful.

The following morning, when he walked into the freezing dining room and saw the rows of white-faced ragged children staring pitifully up at him, each holding a small crust of bread and a glass of cold water, Mr Fox couldn't bear it. Rather than sit with them at breakfast (if

141

you could call it that) he hurried to his study.

"This can't go on," he muttered to himself as he entered – and was amazed to hear a familiar voice replying resonantly, "No, indeed, Mr Fox, it can't!"

There, sitting in front of his desk, with Tom and Miles, was Mr Fritz.

Mr Fritz! Mr Fox's face was a picture. The sight of the teacher and his two pupils filled him with such delight that he felt like dancing and hugging them. And yet he also felt like bursting into tears. His face went blue and red in turn, his eyes shone alternately with relief and delight, his hair seemed to droop and spring at the same time and he shook with emotion.

"My dear Mr Fritz! And Tom and Miles! I have never been so pleased to see anyone in all my life!" he said. And, sinking into his chair, he covered his face with his hands and sobbed.

Mr Fritz turned to Tom and Miles, puzzled. He hadn't been expecting this reaction.

"Pull yourself together, man," said Mr Fritz getting up and slapping him on the back. "And before we start talking, get someone to turn on the heat! The school's freezing!"

Mr Fox obediently pulled his intercom towards him. "Mr Carstairs?" he barked. A rather weak voice could be heard on the other end. "Too cold!" said the headmaster. "Today the heat must go back on!"

"Thank you, Headmaster," came the faint reply. "I'll do it at once."

"Now," said Mr Fritz, going back to his chair and looking extremely severe. "This has got to stop! Tom and Miles have explained what's happened. You've got to stand up to the Phantom. It doesn't matter what he does to the school – forget it. If you continue like this the school will be standing but you'll have deaths on your hands."

"I know, I know!" wailed Mr Fox. "But how can I stand up to the Phantom? He's got such power!"

"We'll think about that later," said Mr Fritz. "In the mean time, I suggest you take assembly and tell the pupils the experiment is over. Everyone must have something good and hot to eat – ring up those caterers we were using before!" he added brusquely.

"And what about the children getting in touch with their parents?" asked Mr Fox nervously.

Mr Fritz sighed. "Quite honestly they should be allowed to be in touch right away. Most of them should be at home recovering, if the few pupils I've seen this morning are an example of what's going on! But I take your point. I suggest you put the heating on high, provide a slap-up meal, give them today off – buy twenty videos, six television sets and six video recorders so everyone can get to see them – give them a huge dinner tonight and congratulate them on a brilliant experiment. Tell them how much it must have made them appreciate what people in other countries go through – and then let them write to their parents or ring them."

"Sneaky!" said Miles.

"Sneaky," said Mr Fritz, "but necessary."

Mr Fox looked at him gratefully. Then his expression changed. "But what are we going to do about the Phantom?" he said. "It's no use us getting everything back to normal if the Phantom just pulls the school down on top of everyone. Everyone might just as well have starved to death!"

"First things first," said Mr Fritz. "I'll organize the caterers and the tellies and so on – you organize assembly."

It was a pathetic group of pupils that faced Mr Fox in the huge hall. Some had to be supported by others, they were so weak; some were so cold they had wound themselves in the sheets from their beds. One had even managed to wrap an enormous canvas wall atlas around himself.

Many of the children's hands were bleeding and scabbed from heaving bricks, and their faces looked worn and hollow.

When they had all assembled in the big hall Mr Fox noticed something very different in the

144

atmosphere. Usually there was a distant muttering of whispering and giggling; but now the
pupils were too tired and worn out to speak.
So there was really no need for Mr Fox to clap
his hands for attention, but he did anyway,
because that was what he always did.

"First of all may I say – congratulations!" he
intoned. "You have all been through a lot these
past weeks and I think we have shown the
world that when it comes to the environment,
Burlap Hall means business. We've learnt a
lot – and starving children in the Third World
have profited by our generosity in donating
half our food to them." (Total lie, but who
cared.) "Caterers are now on their way to provide a steaming hot breakfast for the lot of you
– and you will have the rest of the day off as
the teachers and I start getting the school back
to normal for lessons tomorrow. But this afternoon, we have a selection of televisions and
videos and you may watch what you like.
There will be a large celebratory dinner this
evening as a big thank you for your participa-
tion in this most successful and, may I say it,
educational, event!"

In Mr Fox's study, where Mr Fritz had finished making a mammoth order for food and
treats, the strains of feeble cheers could be
heard as the pupils all weakly showed their
appreciation. A thin verse of "For he's a jolly
good fellow!" started up as Mr Fox was borne

aloft on the shoulders of some of the fitter pupils, back to his study. Mr Carstairs tottered forward rather faintly to shake him by the hand. "A brilliant scheme, Mr Fox! Ecologically, environmentally, globally a constructive and illuminating experiment! A work of genius!"

"A bold and fascinating idea!" said Mr Roy, clasping him by the hand. "It has brought geography alive!"

"I have written a masterpiece during these two weeks," said Signor Ruzzi, giving Mr Fox a bear-hug. "Ballada of the Worlda Thirda. I will play eet for you as soon as possible!"

"Most impressive, Headmaster," murmured Mrs Grain and Miss Shepherd and they tottered past him towards the dining room for breakfast.

Overhearing the compliments in Mr Fox's study, Mr Fritz shook his head at the two boys. "People's memories are so short," he said sighing. "This is how dictators work, you know. Make the masses miserable and then make them happy. Remember that."

Flushed with success from his triumphant speech, Mr Fox was on top form as he took his place again behind his desk. But Mr Fritz soon brought him down to earth. "You ought to be ashamed of yourself, Fox," he said sharply. "The way you have behaved has been unspeakable. Weak, cowardly and cruel. If it hadn't been for my coming back last night you would have probably been up on a charge of mass manslaughter, if not worse. So wipe that smile off your face and start thinking about how we defeat the Phantom!"

Mr Fox, unused to this kind of talk from Mr Fritz, was just about to deliver one of his famous "Looks", but was quelled by a look from Mr Fritz that, in comparison, made his own seem a mere puzzled frown. He changed his "Look" to one of shame. "So what are we going to do?" he asked meekly.

The silence that fell in the office hung like a shroud. Then Tom spoke.

"Perhaps we'd better go back to the beginning," he said.

"Excellent," said Mr Fritz. "I'm glad to see your science lessons have taught you something after all. Yes, the beginning. When was it that the Phantom started to appear?"

Mr Fox racked his brains.

"Well, he didn't send any letters last term," he said.

"No," said Mr Fritz. "And the first letter you had was at the beginning of this term."

"So whatever it was that prompted his coming happened in the holidays," said Miles.

"Nothing much happened in the holidays," said Mr Fox petulantly. "Leaks. Christmas. More leaks. New Year. Central heating broke down. More leaks."

"Drains," added Mr Fritz.

"Ah, yes, drains," said Mr Fox. "In fact, now I think about it, it was just after the drain men had gone that I got the first letter from the Phantom. Yes – it was a matter of hours."

"What was the matter with the drains?" asked Tom. The word instantly reminded him of the smell.

"Blockage," said Mr Fox rather crossly. "Something stuck. Cost a fortune."

"*What* was stuck?" asked Miles.

"God knows. Ask Drain-O-Cure. Except the drain men have probably gone away and bought a small kingdom with the money I paid them."

Mr Fritz was thinking. "The body was never found," he said.

"You mean you think Squooch's body was hidden in the drains?" said Miles.

"But if the pupils hid the body there, the drains would have been blocked always," said Tom. "Unless they chopped it up."

"Then it would have flushed through gradually," said Miles, sensibly but chillingly. "First a finger, then an arm and so on."

"Unless..." said Tom. "Let's see that cutting you got from the paper again, Mr Fritz."

Mr Fritz handed it to him.

"Look," said Tom pointing excitedly. "See that bit about the casket from the church? It was never found, was it?"

"Casket? Church?" Mr Fox looked crossly at Mr Fritz. "Wouldn't you two boys like to go and have some breakfast while Mr Fritz and I discuss the matter?"

Mr Fritz looked furiously at Mr Fox. "I don't think you appreciate quite what a fix we are in, Fox," he snapped. "We need every scrap of help we can get! Particularly from two boys with such fine brains as Miles and Tom!" Tom felt his ears go red as Mr Fritz turned to him. "Please continue. No, the casket was never, to my knowledge, found."

"Well, all I can think is that the pupils of Burlap Hall chopped Mr Squooch up into tiny bits, put his remains in the casket..."

"And hid the casket down the drain!" said Miles triumphantly. "No wonder Horace Squooch or the casket were never found! The boys were so small they could fit down the drain but no adult could ever find the casket because they were too big to crawl down there!"

Mr Fritz rubbed his beard, thoughtfully. "It's a long shot, I must say," he murmured.

"But remember, the first letter came just after the drains had been cleared," said Mr Fox, enthusiastically. "If by unblocking the drains the Drain-O-Cure people actually dislodged the casket and pushed it open, then..."

At this point he rather fizzled out.

"I bet his ghost can only exist if his bones

aren't locked up," said Miles.

Mr Fritz agreed. "Obviously while his bones are still free, the Phantom can wander where he likes."

"And that's why he lives in the drains!" said Tom.

"But if he's a Phantom he can't have bones," said Miles.

Tom looked at him crossly. "Oh, you know. It's all to do with his spirit and so on. It makes sense to me."

"And it's beginning to make sense to me," said Mr Fritz. "It's worth investigating, anyway."

"We've got no other line of inquiry," said Mr Fox, gloomily fiddling with a pencil.

"If we can get the bones and lock them back in the casket, the Phantom will be trapped again," said Mr Fritz.

"Tom is smaller than me," said Miles, knowing what was coming next.

Tom felt his heart sinking to his boots. "Me? Go down into the drains? And collect the Phantom's bones, and put them back in the casket, and lock it, and then come out?"

There was an embarrassed silence.

"We'd be very proud of you, Tom," said Mr Fox, pleadingly.

"I'd still sit next to you even if you smelt like dead rats," said Miles.

"You're our only hope," said Mr Fritz.

Tom sighed. "OK. But promise me one thing."

"What?"

"No one flush the lavatories when I'm down there."

CHAPTER NINE

"So how do we get to these drains?" asked Mr Fritz. They were in the headmaster's study examining an ancient map that Mr Fox had found in an old file, showing the plans for the building, and the drainage system beneath the ground floor which led to the main sewer.

Mr Fox was pursing his lips as he studied it. "This is most odd," he said. "Look."

Tom, Miles and Mr Fritz leaned over and saw for themselves. The drains ran straight out underneath the building, but before they reached the main sewer there was a series of circles and steps that looked like underground caves.

"That's where we saw Susan meeting the Phantom!" said Tom, pointing. "That's where the door must be – the one that Miles and I found. And there are the steps leading down. And there's the first cave – and it looks as if it leads to two others."

"Obviously the drains lead into these natural caves which then lead out to the main sewer," said Miles. "Lucky they didn't build Burlap Hall on top of them! Otherwise it would have caved in!"

At his words there was a long silence. Finally Tom spoke, putting into words something which each of them was thinking.

"Look," he said. "The drains lead first here," – and he pointed to where the science block had been – "and then here," – and he pointed to where the sports centre had been. "They also run under the kitchens."

"And look – there's a small bit of drain that's just under the assembly hall. Just where Signor Ruzzi plays his piano!" breathed Miles.

"So that's how he did it," said Mr Fritz. "He's somehow got into the drains and under the foundations and by loosening them, he's managed to pull down bits of the school!"

Mr Fox seized the map, studying it furiously. "Let's see that! What else is there? Oh, my goodness! The whole of the west wing! That's got a huge bit of drain under it. That's what he was planning next!"

Mr Fritz sprang into action. "Evacuate it," he ordered. "Clear everyone from it. At once."

"But surely he wouldn't..."

"It's not worth the risk, Headmaster," said Mr Fritz. "Please get everyone out for the moment. If that collapses all the children will be killed instantly."

"Well, let's get Tom down the drains first, and do that afterwards," said Mr Fox. "There might be no need."

"I'm not going down any drains until the west wing's evacuated," said Tom firmly. "Mr Fritz is right."

"But it will take ages!" said Mr Fox, despairingly. "And it's nearly lunchtime as it is!"

But Tom stood firm, so for the next three hours they organized the move – a demanding job since it involved everyone packing up, posters being taken off walls, plus any good bits of furniture and pictures being heaved across the building from one side to the other. Mr Fritz insisted the new carpet be taken up as well, just in case. Had the children been a bit fitter it might have been quicker, but they were all still weak, even after their hearty breakfast. It was five o'clock by the time everyone was comfortably settled, rather higgledy-piggledy, in the east wing. But at least they'd had a big lunch. The blankets had been retrieved and everyone had somewhere cosy to sleep for the night; it was toasty warm as everyone settled down to a good night's goggling and eating.

"It's getting dark," said Tom to Miles as they came out of their room, having shoved their beds up to share with Simon and Asquith Minor. "I hope Mr Fox won't want me to go down into the drains now."

"We'll have to wait till tomorrow," said Miles. "You can't go down at night. Hey – I haven't seen Susan recently, have you? Do you think she's still in her room studying?"

"That's a point," said Tom. "Let's see."

But to their surprise, they found Susan's

door wide open and a gaggle of people inside munching crisps and watching *Raiders of the Lost Ark* on one of the new television sets.

"Have you seen Susan?" asked Tom.

"Sssh!" said everyone. But Rosemary piped up, "No, it's rather odd. About half an hour ago she got up and walked out without saying a word. She just handed me this."

She rummaged round on Susan's desk and came up with a yellowish piece of parchment, folded over.

"Let's see that!" cried Tom, seizing it. "It's the Phantom, I'm sure!"

"The who?" said Rosemary.

"Sssh!" said everyone.

Tom took the letter outside. Written on it were the words: "To whom it may concern". He opened it and read the message aloud to Miles.

I HAVE THE GIRL, he read. *You are fools not to listen to my warnings. You have gone too far this time. Mr Fox will live to regret his actions as you will discover tonight!*
Yours,
The Phantom

"He's got Susan!" cried Miles. "We must do something!"

Together they raced down the corridors to Mr Fox's office. "Sir, sir!" they cried, bursting in and showing him the letter.

Mr Fox's face went white when he read it. He immediately summoned Mr Fritz. "This is terrible, Fritz," he said. "I told you we should have acted sooner."

"No, no," said Mr Fritz. "This threat – he means the west wing. It's the only thing left he can touch – you can see on the map! There's no time to be lost!"

"What if we're wrong and there're no bones or casket in the drains?" said Tom.

"I'll go after Susan," said Miles. "I remember the way."

"But you don't have a boat!" said Tom. "You won't be able to follow her!"

"Boat?" said Mr Fox. "Are you all going completely crazy?"

"You need a boat, if there's water," said Mr Fritz.

"Here," said Mr Fox, pulling up a battered old tray from the side of his desk and handing it to Miles. "This'll be better than nothing. And – and you can use these as oars." He handed him a couple of rulers which Miles took, rather dubiously. "Now, off you go – and good luck!"

Miles gulped and hesitated slightly.

"I'll do it, if you want to go down the drains instead," said Tom.

"Er ... no," said Miles. "I'll go. See you." And, putting on a brave face, he left to carry out his mission.

"Now, let's find the best access point for these drains," said Mr Fritz, looking at the map with a magnifying glass.

Tom stared as well. "Look!" he said. "There's a little circle with MHC written by it!"

"But what does that mean?" asked Mr Fox.

"Man-hole cover," said Tom.

"Good lad!" cried Mr Fritz. "Now, let's go!"

Armed with a torch they left the school (Tom having insisted that Mr Carstairs be told that no one could have a bath, wash up or use the loo for the next couple of hours), and searched the grounds for the man-hole cover. They found it overgrown with ivy, just to the left of the gravel path leading from the Hall. Using a spade, Mr Fritz dug frantically around the edges and finally lifted it.

There was a narrow, dark hole dropping, as far as they could see, straight down into the earth. A few iron rungs were lodged into the wall of the tunnel, but the beam of the torch didn't reach the bottom. All that they could see was pitch darkness. All they could hear was a faint glugging sound of water. And all they could smell was – "Phew!" said Tom. "Anyone got a clothes peg?"

"You'd better hurry," said Mr Fox, rather unsympathetically. "Otherwise..."

Gingerly, Tom took the torch and, wriggling down into the hole, found the first rung. Holding the torch in his teeth, he started to descend.

"Good luck!" called Mr Fritz from above. "Take care!"

"Ungh, ungh," replied Tom through the torch, as he stepped down and down, until eventually he could see nothing above him, but a very faint, pale circle of evening light.

Ugh! It was horrible down here! The rungs were slimy, rats' eyes stared at him from crevices in the tunnel, and it was bitterly, bitterly cold. Those bones had better be there, thought Tom. If he was doing all this for nothing – well!

Miles wasn't having a much better time. He'd found the door to the caverns, gone down the steps and gingerly balanced his tray on the black water at the bottom. Luckily, it had raised sides or the water would surely have come in, but at least the pond was completely calm, and as long as he kept his nerve and his balance he felt reasonably secure. He climbed slowly on to the tray, and, with a ruler, pushed off from the quay.

There was only one direction to go – the way he'd seen the Phantom take Susan, over to the other side of the cave and through a craggy split in the rocks. Holding his breath, he paddled across using his hands – the rulers proved useless – until he reached the other side. He really didn't feel like going through the rocky arch – but there was Susan to think of. If he didn't go, who knew what might happen to her? He pressed on, into the bitter blackness, lowering his head to avoid bumping the jagged rocks above, until he emerged on the other side.

Here was yet another cave, much the same as the first. Of Susan or the Phantom, there was absolutely no sign.

But a single candle glowed over on a rocky ledge, on the opposite side to where he'd come in. This was some sign of life, at least. Candles didn't just light themselves on their own, after all. Feeling a little encouraged, Miles paddled over to the candle and looked around. Still nothing. And, worse, there seemed no way out of this cave, though he remembered on the map that there were three caverns in all. What baffled him was how on earth to get into the third.

Then he heard a very faint voice.

"No! No!" it cried. It was Susan.

Tom, meanwhile, had reached the bottom of the man-hole and was now inching his way along the smallest, slimiest, muddiest, most revolting tunnel he could imagine. His hands and feet were freezing, and the tunnel was so narrow that he could only squeeze himself along a few centimetres at a time. In order to have his hands free, he had to hold the torch in his mouth again, the beam pointing outward to light the tunnel ahead. It looked endless. How would he ever manage to get back, he wondered? What if Mr Carstairs forgot to tell everyone about the baths and so on and some-one pulled a plug and he drowned? His heart pounded. Don't panic, he told himself. Keep calm. If there were rungs on the hole coming down, someone must have been here before. But if only he hadn't eaten such a big Chinese meal the night before and such a huge lunch, he was sure he could have made better progress.

On and on he went, until suddenly the torch lit up something strange ahead of him. Wrig-gling along furiously in his efforts to see what it was, and scraping his shins and knees painfully on the stones, he finally arrived at the object.

There, jutting from a ledge where it seemed trapped, was a casket. It was covered with green slime and barnacles and wiggly things. And, making Tom's heart leap, the lid was missing.

Tom held his breath with excitement. Now all he had to find were the bones!

Back in the second cave, Miles was frantic with worry. He could hear Susan's voice, pleading. But still he could find no way to reach her. Round and round he paddled, three times at least, each time feeling more and more useless. He heard Susan begin to cry. Then a horrible dead, dark voice said, "There is no alternative, my dear. You are mine!"

Taking a grip on himself, Miles stopped paddling. This was getting him nowhere. He felt weak and dizzy with paddling. Think, Miles! Think! he urged himself.

Looking round the cave once more, he tried to calm down and assess the situation. The only way into the third cave had to be via some tunnel lower down, underwater. But how had the Phantom and Susan got there, if you had to swim through an underwater hole? It didn't make sense. And yet he felt that must be the only answer. He made his way back to where the candle flickered, and stared with his torch into the water.

There, just below the waterline, was indeed a large hole. Miles was just about to jump off his tea tray and swim into it when he paused. How long was the tunnel? He didn't want to drown in there. He had to be sure it was a short one before he started off or he'd be done for. He looked around again. And then, suddenly, just above the candle, he spotted a lever. Hesitating, he pulled it down. There was a grinding of machinery and a sucking noise, and slowly the water beneath him dropped lower and lower.

It was a lock system, like they had on canals!

161

It had to be! There was no other explanation. The water sank right down until the tunnel was completely exposed and Miles could sail right through it. But then he heard the Phantom shouting angrily.

"What is the meaning of this? The water is rising! Someone must be in Cavern Two! I must rectify this at once!"

And just as Miles was getting to the end of the tunnel, he heard the machinery grind into action again. The Phantom must be pulling a lever in the third cave which would flood the tunnel again. In the darkness Miles wriggled faster and faster. Eventually the water rose so high that there was less than a metre between it and the roof of the tunnel. The tea tray fell away underneath him and he was forced to swim. Faster and faster he swam, and faster and faster the water rose, until his head was grazing the top of the tunnel. Then, taking a deep breath, he mentally crossed his fingers, plunged underwater and swam with all his might till he finally made it to the other side. Bursting for air he shot, gasping, to the surface.

It was some time before Miles could get his bearings. He was now in the third cave. And across from him, on the other side, another candle glowed lighting up a vast library of books set into the walls. Its light also illuminated two figures, standing on a rocky ledge:

Susan, pale and trembling, and the Phantom, still pressing the lever. As he saw Miles, he released his grip.

Dressed in black he looked like a giant – a huge black cloak of evil that towered over poor Susan and shook with rage as he focussed his attention on Miles.

"So!" he intoned. "You have pursued me! That was not a very sensible idea, my friend!" And the Phantom's menacing chuckle echoed round the walls.

"Susan!" said Miles desperately. "Are you all right?"

Susan looked dazed, hardly able to comprehend that he was there. "Oh, Miles!" she said.

The Phantom took her by the hand and forced her to look at him. "You are my best pupil. I have taken you under my wing. You are now mine and we will be together for ever. You will soon become the cleverest person in the whole world and then, my dear, you and I will rule it together. Education is a marvellous thing. And education gives us power – power over subnormal ninnies like him!" And with that he whirled round and pointed at Miles.

Through the slits in his black hood, Miles could see his eyes shimmering with evil.

"Well?" cackled the Phantom. "Aren't you coming to collect your friend?"

Miles hesitated, treading water. Then he struck out towards the rocky bank.

"Ha ha!" cried the Phantom, screaming with laughter and stepping to the edge of the water. "How do you think you are going to land?" With that he pulled a long sharp glittering knife from his cloak and brandished it in the air. "No, my foolish friend. You will be unable to land because I will cut your fingers to pieces before you can get a grip! And you will be unable to swim back without drowning because that passage is far too long. So you will simply swim and swim in this pond until you die. It should take about twelve hours. Perhaps twenty-four. But don't worry. Susan and I have all the time in the world!"

Meanwhile, Tom had taken a temporary rest. He needed to think, and think carefully. If the bones were scattered about, how would he carry them all? He really should have brought a plastic bag. The only thing he could gather them in was the casket. But it was awfully big and bulky. He would have to wriggle past the casket, find the bones and bring back as many as possible in one go. The drain had widened slightly at this point, so Tom was able to move slightly more freely though he still found it hard to turn round. But first things first. Tom wriggled into the tunnel ahead.

It seemed a hopeless task. The drain stretched ahead on and on, revealing nothing. But as he moved, something scratched him.

Wiggling back, he looked at the side of the wall again. Trapped in a small crevice was what seemed to be a white stick. Tom pulled at it – it was a bone! He found another, then another and another – five in all. They were unmistakably finger bones. He found more bones attached – wrist, fore-arm and upper arm. He gathered them up as best he could and scrabbled back to the casket.

Back in the water, Miles considered his position. The Phantom seemed to have him well and truly trapped. But there was no way he was going to give up without a fight. No way! Bravely, he struck out for the rocky bank, trying not to think of the consequences.

As he got nearer, the Phantom rushed towards Miles, the dagger held high in his hand. Tensing himself for the cut, Miles stretched out a hand to the shore. But at the very moment that the creature prepared to thrust the dagger into Miles' hand, the Phantom's arm seemed suddenly to disappear. The cloak flopped down and the knife fell straight into the water.

The Phantom cursed and staggered. "What are they doing to me?" he muttered. "The fools!"

Encouraged by this, Miles reached out again for the shore. But just as the Phantom's foot was about to crash down on to his hand – the foot, too, suddenly disappeared. Then, amazingly, the Phantom collapsed on to the ground.

"The fiends!" he muttered, dragging himself to where his boat was moored and seizing an oar to use as a crutch. The grotesque black cripple came hopping back, but he was too slow for Miles, who had taken the opportunity to spring ashore and rush to Susan's side.

"Tom's done it!" he shouted. "He's found the bones!"

It was at the moment that Tom found a whitened skull that the Phantom's head disappeared. The cloak dropped on to his shoulders and this headless black monster limped wildly, veering from side to side.

Trembling, Miles put a hand round Susan's shoulders. He guided her to the lever which the Phantom had pulled, and pushed it upwards. The Phantom couldn't see anything now, nor could he speak, but it was a deformed, fury-packed creature that hobbled around, feeling the way along the walls with one arm.

"Look, the water's going down, Susan," said Miles. "Jump in with me and we can swim to safety!"

"Oh, Miles, thank goodness you came!" said Susan. "I don't know what would have happened otherwise!"

"Jump!" ordered Miles. Together they leapt into the black water and swam to the under-

166

ground tunnel, leaving what was left of the Phantom raging on the shore. Just as they dived for the tunnel, Miles looked back. The creature was feeling its way around the walls. With a superhuman wrench from its one good arm, it detached a slab of rock – and, accompanied by an enormous explosion, the whole of the cavern roof collapsed into the water. Above it, the west wing of Burlap Hall rocked unsteadily – and then fell in a heap.

"Swim!" shouted Miles, pushing Susan through the tunnel. "Swim for your life!"

CHAPTER TEN

Although Tom felt the tremor underground, he couldn't work out what it was. He continued with his bone-collecting, wriggling along the drain until he finally came across the spinal column, broken in half to fit into the casket. Squirming backwards, he managed to stuff all the bones inside the box. Then he took stock of the situation. The drain was just too small for him to turn in, and he could hardly wriggle backwards all the way he'd come. It would take hours. So backing up, he heaved the casket from the ledge and shoved it forward in front of him, planning to continue until he came to another man-hole cover. There must be one soon, he thought.

On and on he wriggled, wondering all the time if he were doing the right thing and whether he shouldn't have gone backwards after all. Perhaps he'd come to the main sewer eventually and be carried away on a river of other people's bathwater and who knew what else? But just as he was despairing of ever reaching Burlap Hall again, he heard someone calling his name. It was only faint but it was definitely human.

"Yes! Yes! I'm here!" yelled Tom, his voice echoing strangely. He was suffused with relief. He intensified his efforts, struggling on and on, pushing slowly, and as he moved he became aware that the voice was Mr Fritz's. "Here, Tom, here!" called Mr Fritz. Briefly turning off his torch, Tom could make out another patch of light ahead.

"I'm here, Mr Fritz! I've got the bones!" called Tom. And the word "bones" sounded like "BOWOWONNZZZ!"

"Come along! That's great!" shouted back Mr Fritz, and eventually Tom's endless tunnel was broken by a long shaft up to the air.

"I've got the bones and the casket but I can't carry them up!" yelled Tom.

"Hold on, I'll get some rope," shouted Mr Fritz.

He disappeared and Mr Fox's voice came booming down. "Well done!" he shouted. "But I'm afraid you were too late to save the west wing. It's collapsed!"

"Oh no, sir," said Tom. He rather wished Mr Fox could have waited till he'd got up to tell him the news.

A few minutes later the casket, bones and Tom were all hoisted to ground level with the help of the rope. Mr Fritz shook his hand and then reeled back.

"Well dud!" he said. "But I thick a bath would be id order!"

"Oh dear, is it that bad?" said Tom, rubbing himself. "But I could do with a bath, I must say. Will you deal with the bones?"

169

"I certainly will," said Mr Fritz, keeping his distance. "The vicar's planning a special burial that will see that Horace Squooch rests in peace from now on. He's thrilled to get his casket back. Too bad you didn't manage to find the lid," he added as he took it.

"Well, I'm certainly not going back to look for it," said Tom, making for the school. "If the vicar wants his lid he can go and look for it himself! It's horrible down there!"

Miles and Susan got to the first cave shivering with cold and fear. Together they scrambled up the slippery steps and hand in hand made their way through the woods to the school.

"He's pulled down the west wing," said Miles, seeing the smoking ruins. "Oh, dear. That's the end of Burlap Hall."

"Still, you saved my life," said Susan, giving him a quick peck on the cheek which made Miles blush in the dark. "And I'll never forget that, Miles."

They slipped in to Burlap Hall to find Tom in a furious temper with Mr Carstairs.

"But I *must* have a bath!" he was saying. "I'm the *reason* no one could have baths. But it's all over now. I'm freezing. And I smell to high ... oh, hello!"

He suddenly noticed Miles and Susan, both sopping wet, standing at the door. Susan rushed over to him. "And you saved my life,

170

too!" she said, giving him a big hug. But the moment she had put her arms round him she sprang away. "Ugh!" she said. "The smell!"

"You can talk!" said Tom, holding his nose. "Come on, we're all going to have baths whatever you say," he added to Mr Carstairs in a fit of courage, pushing the teacher from the door of the bathrooms. "Mr Fritz says it's fine now."

"Oh, well, if Mr Fritz says so," said Mr Carstairs, backing away as the three of them approached him. "Thed go ahead."

Now thoroughly cleaned up, the friends had been asked by Mr Fox to go to his study for a special thanks. It was a bit of a bore because they were just about to watch a new Disney cartoon after a huge supper. "But I suppose we'll have to," said Tom.

"I expect he'll give us book tokens or something," said Miles.

"Oh, no, not book tokens," said Susan. "I never want to see another book in my life."

"I wonder if you'll remember all the knowledge the Phantom pumped into you?" said Tom as they walked down the corridor.

"No," said Susan. "I can feel it all seeping away from me."

"Pity," said Miles. "It would have been nice to have got something out of it."

"I've got a lot out of it," said Susan. "I now

know I've got two of the best friends in the world."

"Oh, it was nothing," said Tom and Miles awkwardly. "Any time."

"He must have hypnotized me all those evenings," said Susan. "Because I can't really remember any of it now. Except that I used to feel I *had* to go to the woods and down those stairs. Then he'd give me these lessons."

"Don't think about it," advised Miles.

Mr Fox was plunged in gloom when they got to his office. Mr Fritz was looking depressed, too, though he was trying to put a brave face on it.

When they came in Mr Fox got up.

"I wanted to thank you personally," he said, "because I don't know when I'll be seeing you all again."

"Sir?" said Tom.

"You see, Tom," said Mr Fox, "the west wing has finally collapsed. That means that the place cannot really continue to function as a school. The insurance company has turned down my claims and insist that what has occurred is just an Act of God. It looks as if next term you will all be at different schools. And so will Mr Fritz and I, if we are lucky enough to find jobs. This," he intoned, close to tears, "is the end of Burlap Hall as we know it."

"But sir, surely not – just as things were

going so well at the beginning of term!" said Susan. "We were the most advanced school in the country! With our new science block."

"And our sports centre," said Miles.

"And everything else," said Tom, not knowing what to add.

"But you see," said Mr Fritz. "We can't afford to rebuild it. The insurance company won't pay. They've examined every map and every clause in our insurance policy and they refuse."

"Rubbish!" said Tom.

"Tom!" said Mr Fritz.

"Sorry, sir, but rubbish," said Tom, again. "I bet you haven't shown them that map of the drains, have you?"

There was an extremely long silence. Mr Fox felt the tips of his fingers starting to tingle. Mr Fritz's hairy suit seemed to come alive. Both their faces became flushed with suppressed excitement.

Then, "Well done!" exploded Mr Fox, finally. "You're right! – you've got more drains than all of us put together!"

"Brains!" shouted Mr Fritz. "Brains! Tom, you're brilliant!"

"As long you show them that map..." said Tom.

"I will!" said Mr Fox.

"And as long as the drains are covered by the insurance..." said Miles.

"They are!" squealed Mr Fox happily.

"And as long as you can get some engineer to come along and prove it, which can't be difficult..." said Susan.

"Then we're covered!" said Mr Fritz. He seized Mr Fox's hands and led him in a dance around the room.

"Have a drink, boys!" said Mr Fox as he danced.

"And girls," sang Mr Fritz.

"Have some book tokens as well! Help yourself to as many as you want. They're in the top drawer!" said Mr Fox.

"Actually, maybe we could just go back and watch telly," said Miles.

"Anything you want!" said Mr Fox and Mr Fritz. "Tell any teachers you see, by the way, to come along here. We're going to open a bottle of champagne!"

"Two bottles!" said Mr Fox. "No, let's make it three!"

"What a day," said Tom as they drank Coke in a corner of the common room, having watched three films in succession. Asquith Minor was arguing with Simon, who hadn't understood one of the films, and was laboriously explaining the plot to him.

"Oh, I bet your knees are all sore with wriggling down drains," said Susan, who was now completely normal.

"Nothing to what you went through," said Tom, loyally.

"She brought it all on herself," said Miles. "If she hadn't gone out looking for that *Rights for Kids!* book in the middle of the night she would never have got caught up in it."

"I'll tell you something," said Susan, leaning forward. "When you're sixteen you can buy cigarettes, tobacco and cigarette papers and a young person is allowed to smoke at any age *but* if you're under sixteen and caught by a uniformed policeman or park keeper, they can seize your tobacco and cigarette papers but *not* your pipe or tobacco. Isn't that weird?"

"Is that *Rights for Kids!* or Phantom?" asked Miles. (Susan glared at him.) "Anyway, we should be glad Susan looked for her book because otherwise Mr Fox would have met the Phantom without us knowing anything about it and we'd probably all be dead by now."

"Honestly – Mr Fox," said Tom. "He's just as bad as Horace Squooch in his own way."

"Not quite," said Susan. "I think he was hypnotized a bit, like me."

"And anyway," said Miles. "If anyone ever thinks of rising up and killing Mr Fox, they should remember one thing…"

Tom grinned. "Don't hide his bones in the drains!" he said.